THE SMALLER SKY

JOHN WAIN was born in 1925 in Stoke-on-Trent, Staffordshire. He attended St John's College, Oxford, earning a BA in 1946 and an MA in 1950. A prolific author and man of letters, Wain wrote poetry, novels, criticism, and biographies during a writing career that spanned more than forty years.

He started out teaching at the University of Reading, but in 1953 left to pursue writing full-time. Wain's first novel, *Hurry on Down* (1953; published in the United States as *Born in Captivity*) was a bestseller and launched Wain's career as a novelist. The book ran into several hardcover printings and was often reprinted as a Penguin paperback; it is credited with paving the way for later British classics of the 1950s, including Kingsley Amis's *Lucky Jim* (1954) and John Braine's *Room at the Top* (1957). Wain followed his first novel with a number of other novels and short story collections, including *Living in the Present* (1955), *The Contenders* (1958), *A Travelling Woman* (1959), *Strike the Father Dead* (1962), *The Young Visitors* (1965), *Nuncle, and Other Stories* (1965), and *Death of the Hind Legs, and Other Stories* (1966). A number of contemporary critics felt some of these works represented a falling-off from his successful debut novel, but his next novel, *The Smaller Sky* (1967), was well received, and is arguably Wain's masterpiece. Among his later fiction, *A Winter in the Hills* (1970) and *Young Shoulders* (1982) were particularly well regarded; the latter novel won the Whitbread Award.

In 1973, Wain was appointed the first Professor of Poetry at Oxford University, and the following year his biography of Samuel Johnson won the James Tait Black Memorial Prize. His services to literature were recognized in 1984 when he was awarded a CBE. In the late 1980s, he began his 'Oxford Trilogy' with *Where the Rivers Meet* (1988), and the final volume, *Hungry Generations*, was published shortly after his death in 1994.

ALICE FERREBE is Senior Lecturer in English at Liverpool John Moores University. She is the author of *Masculinity in Male-Authored Fiction 1950-2000* (Palgrave Macmillan, 2005) and *Literature of the 1950s: Good, Brave Causes* (Edinburgh University Press, 201~)

GW00538259

By John Wain

* Available from Valancourt Books

JOHN WAIN

The Smaller Sky

With a new introduction by
ALICE FERREBE

𝕶𝖆𝖓𝖘𝖆𝖘 𝕮𝖎𝖙𝖞:
VALANCOURT BOOKS
2013

The Smaller Sky by John Wain
First published London: Macmillan 1967
First Valancourt Books edition 2013

Copyright © 1967 by John Wain
Introduction © 2013 by Alice Ferrebe

Published by Valancourt Books, Kansas City, Missouri
Publisher & Editor: JAMES D. JENKINS
20th Century Series Editor: SIMON STERN, University of Toronto
http://www.valancourtbooks.com

All rights reserved. The use of any part of this publication
reproduced, transmitted in any form or by any means, electronic,
mechanical, photocopying, recording, or otherwise, or stored
in a retrieval system, without prior written consent of the
publisher, constitutes an infringement of the copyright law.

Library of Congress Cataloging-in-Publication Data

Wain, John.
The smaller sky / by John Wain ; with a new introduction
by Alice Ferrebe. – First Valancourt Books edition.
pages ; cm. – (20th century series)
ISBN 978-1-939140-34-0 *(acid free paper)*
I. Title.
PR6045.A249S55 2013
821'.914–dc23
2013008117

All Valancourt Books publications are printed on acid free paper
that meets all ANSI standards for archival quality paper.

Cover art by Claire Brankin
Set in Dante MT 11/13.5

INTRODUCTION

AGED forty-five, Arthur Geary resigns from his job at the Institute, leaves his wife and children, and goes to live on London's Paddington Station. The potential headlines are irresistible: 'the lonely man who came back from the frontiers of knowledge'; 'Well-known scientist at home only among the journeying'. Adrian Swarthmore, who has not yet made it big enough in Consolidated Television Limited, certainly finds them so. His entrance with camera crew in tow into John Wain's novel *The Smaller Sky*, first published in 1967, is unambiguously that of the villain of the piece. Geary's own role is far more intricate, as a man adrift in a rapidly changing Britain. Bereft of the moral certainties of war and Empire, the nation's energies have been directed elsewhere, and the 'lion's roar [...] drowned out by the louder roar of juke-boxes'. Gazing at a row of metal stools in the station's refreshment room, Geary decides they 'yield up the whole secret of the modern mass society. You can't move the stools about the room, they are fixed in their exact equidistance, but you can revolve them. Limited freedom! Naught for your comfort, all for your convenience!' Swarthmore is Wain's creature of this spinning, swinging, mass society, 'plugged in to the mind of the public *now*, this minute', and concerned only with the whirl of publicity. That he communicates his pursuit of Geary's story in terms of atavistic urges only emphasises his own artifice. 'It was no light thing', he believes, 'to hunt a man in order to mount his head above your fireplace'.

In contrast, Geary's is a sylvan quest, not a safari. At first, Paddington Station is to him 'the forest glade where he had made his legitimate home'. It has soaring glass domes with wrought iron parameters (framing that 'smaller sky'), and life flows ceaselessly through it; it is a transitional space between city and country in which Geary can feel anonymous and secure. When it starts to snow, the station becomes 'as tranquil as a thatched cottage': Geary's is a very English idyll, and Paddington a great British building, designed by Isambard Kingdom Brunel, civil architect and enduring civic luminary. Yet the vicissitudes of national change cannot be excluded by its arches. In the station which was the first footfall in London for so many immigrants during the postwar boom, racial antagonism lurks in fraught encounters with bigoted, violent Irishmen, and West Indian café workers diligently clear tables to move customers on, so that to a prickly Geary, his empty coffee cup 'stood at his elbow like some defiant symbol of an Englishman's liberty'. Part of the pathos is that the nostalgic nation Geary longs for no longer exists – and perhaps never did.

We are given few specifics as to the protagonist's appearance beyond his grey tweed cap, told only that he is 'the typical image of a quiet middle-aged man'. There is a hint that his scientific work immediately after the Second World War, upon which Geary was silenced by the Official Secrets Act, may have contributed to his seeking sanctuary in the station. However, such a direct conclusion was contradicted in an interview with Wain in which he cast Geary in a more universal role, claiming that, although his character would have experienced certain pressures in his position as a scientist, these pressures exist in all professions: 'I might have made him a poet if it comes to that'[1]. Geary himself sums up the emotional implications of contemporary Britain more starkly: 'I don't think anybody's all right.' The Smaller Sky, Wain suggested in the same interview, was 'not to use a dangerous word – a symbolic nouvelle about loneliness'. The 'dangerous word' is unspecified: it could be the exotic import 'nouvelle', the short novel form (more respected in literary traditions across the English Channel), it could refer to symbolism (ditto), or it could be 'loneliness'. This is certainly Geary's immediate and presiding danger, but Wain does not confine it to the sensibility of his central character. Philip Robinson, Geary's former colleague, is lonely amidst the bustle of his suburban household – he fears a similar deprivation in his young son. And in the portrayal of ten-year-old David Geary, Wain's symbolism, and his pathos, reach their peak. Across the Pond, sixteen years previously, Holden Caulfield had sought out the ducks in New York's Central Park as metaphors of the mysteries of adult life. David's visits to the duck-pond in a London commuter-belt park, with his judicious and compassionate doling of stale bread, allow him a rare certainty that 'in one small spot of the universe, one round pond with stiff reeds, kindness and justice would rule. He would tell his father that. He would like that idea.' 'All You Need is Love', hymned the Beatles in the year *The Smaller Sky* was published, but paternal love in the novel, though deeply and poignantly felt, is not enough to protect a son from the agonies of the modern world.

Geary's quiet desperation is initially soothed by 'the sleep-walking, incurious crowds of the main-line station'. Yet as the novel continues, his psychiatric state shifts from a Thoreauvian diagnosis to one more akin to the approach of R. D. Laing, who published *The Divided Self* in 1960. His debut study was subtitled 'An Existential Study in Sanity and Madness', which would not be out of place on the cover of *The Smaller Sky*. Laing urged a compassionate understanding of the 'comprehensible transition from the sane schizoid way of being-in-the-world to a psychotic way of being-in-the-world', during which an individual's relation with others and with himself is rent so that 'he experiences himself in despairing aloneness and isolation; moreover, he does not experience himself as a complete person but rather as "split" in various ways'[2]. Swarthmore's self is irreparably divided, his brand of madness a boon in his hypocritical profession. Laing's own anti-psychiatric work became increasingly publicised, and by 1967, in *The Politics of Experience and The Bird of Paradise*, he was preaching of the 'madman' as a seer in an insane world. Wain does not allow Geary such a role. The man's outer calm, we gradually learn, conceals a thudding anxiety, a panicked encounter with the extreme ontological insecurity that postwar continental Existentialist philosophy seeks to confront.

Britain, of course, never experienced Occupation, and in England, existential disorientation was a more muted affair. Born in 1925 in Stoke-on-Trent, Staffordshire, a region where industry focused upon pottery and coal-mining, John Wain had experienced a social mobility that was no less vertiginous for being fairly commonplace in an increasingly affluent Britain. His father worked his way from poverty to become a dentist, and John, via school and the

Officers' Training Corps, went to Oxford, then to the University of Reading as a lecturer in 1947. *Hurry on Down*, his first novel, came out in 1953 (it was published as *Born in Captivity* in the U.S.); in 1955 he became a full-time writer, and went on to hold various visiting professorships in Britain, the States and France. Richard Hoggart, prominent and eloquent analyst of the society of the postwar years in Britain, predicted in 1957 that Wain would become 'a modern man of letters'[3]. So he did, authoring volumes of criticism, poetry, and fiction, as well as television and radio dramas, until his death in 1994. With *Hurry on Down*, a novel of energetic and often contradictory class aspirations, Wain gained himself, for better or worse, the then fashionable literary label of 'Angry Young Man'. His part-autobiography *Sprightly Running* reveals a childhood fraught by the resentment of schoolmates and schoolmasters for his 'posh' family home. His school experience, he claimed, taught him: '(i) that the world was dangerous; (ii) that it was not possible to evade these dangers by being inoffensive [...]; (iii) that, although the natural reaction to all this was fear, I could not admit to feeling fear or I should be disgraced'[4]. By the time of writing *The Smaller Sky*, anger at this enduring injustice is no longer so rawly expressed by the (anti-) hero as it is in Wain's earlier novels. Yet it does persist in his portrayal of that searing loneliness and lack of control experienced both by Geary and his son: a patrilineal despair.

The novel is not innocent of the abiding misogyny of postwar British culture. Wain's female characters are, for the most part, an unedifying bunch, busy with gossip, timely meals and fashionable skirt lengths, and expressing themselves almost 'entirely in shop-worn clichés'. Men (and boys), he suggests, are the lightning rods of the anxiety of contemporary society, while women seem oblivious to all but immediate consumption. However, Elizabeth Geary, Arthur's abandoned wife, does emerge as an increasingly nuanced character. She is offered a glimpse of sympathy for her married life with a man whose 'energy flowed inward', and though she is 'oppressed and intoxicated' by Swarthmore (a neat summation of the seductive effects of mass culture), she rallies admirably in a memorably unpleasant scene in which Wain mutates his villain from cartoonish media whore to real sexual threat.

Elizabeth's point of view is one of seven presented by the novel's third-person narration, and Wain cuts seventeen times between these seven characters. Laing had claimed that 'an authentic science of persons has hardly got started by reason of the inveterate tendency to depersonalize or reify persons'[5], and though Wain's muted pessimism refutes Laing's messianic ring, he too is intent upon demonstrating the complexity of selves and their different subjectivities. Swarthmore has a vision of himself 'welding the shots together with a commentary' to produce his sensationalist documentary, but the novel's narrative gives its readers no clear ideological guidance, and allows no such binding ontological security. Wain was accepting of Marshall McLuhan's suggestion that, during the 1960s, the *Zeitgeist* had left literature and moved instead to film and television, yet he remained cautiously hopeful of a future literary resurgence: 'I don't think the electronic conditions are going to make against language forever'[6]. It is the glare of that 'cruel, impersonal instrument' the camera that drives Geary to the snow-clad edge of his sanity. Yet Wain's deft and decorous intercutting emphasises the subtlety of a literary medium that allows such an ambiguity of character and of message. This delicate strength endures until the novel's enigmatic ending, which holds, as one contemporary critic put it, just 'the right degree of inevitability'[7].

ALICE FERREBE
Liverpool John Moores University

May 29, 2013

1 Peter Firchow, ed., 'John Wain', *The Writer's Place: Interviews on the Literary Situation in Contemporary Britain* (Minneapolis: University of Minnesota Press, 1974), pp. 313-330, 326.
2 R. D. Laing, *The Divided Self* (London: Penguin, 2010), 17.
3 *Nation* 185 (26 Oct 1957), 285.
4 John Wain, *Sprightly Running* (London: Macmillan, 1965), 6.
5 *The Divided Self*, 23.
6 *The Writer's Place*, 324.
7 George Clive, 'New Novels: Desert Victory', *Spectator* 219 (October 6, 1967), 398.

THE SMALLER SKY

Anne's

A S THE high steel arches of the station came into sight, the train slowed, but inside its coaches the tempo of life quickened. People who had sat tranquilly reading, or talking in quiet voices, suddenly began to glance fretfully out of the window, to gather their belongings, to stand up and pull on their overcoats. For sixty-five miles the train had run at an even pace, and now its slowing came as something new and dramatic, the prelude to events that could not be foreseen.

From the crisp autumn light outside, the train nosed smoothly in to the permanent twilight of the station. Before its wheels had stopped turning, doors began to inch open, and the instant it came to rest every door was pushed open wide and a discreetly hurrying crowd spilt out on to the platform under the high glass ceiling. One of the least conspicuous of this crowd was a tall man in a dark-grey overcoat hiding a suit of the same colour. His face showed thoughtfulness and a certain reined-in benevolence; his dark-green felt hat sheltered a long skull, with greying hair crowned by a tiny patch of baldness.

This man now approached the row of benches in the station foyer. He was making for the entrance to the underground railway when his swift footsteps slowed and a polite, enquiring smile appeared on his face. He had recognized an acquaintance. Going up to a man of his own age, dressed in a mackintosh and grey tweed cap, he said cheerfully, 'Hello, Arthur!'

Ten years earlier he would have said 'Hello, Geary!' But, amenable in all social matters, he had moved with the social tide that has caused Englishmen to address one another by their Christian names on no very intimate acquaintance. The man addressed, who had been sitting with folded arms, apparently lost in thought, looked up, recognized him, and said, 'Hello, Philip! Just got off the train?'

'Yes; have you?'

'No,' said Geary. He added nothing further, merely looking up pleasantly at his interlocutor and waiting for him to speak next.

'Well,' said the other. He hesitated. 'Have you time for a cup of coffee? I often have one at the station. It's a better cup than you get on the train, besides being cheaper.'

'Provided you get it on Platform One,' said Geary gravely, 'where they make it properly. The stuff out of the urn in the other place is worse than anything on the trains. But yes,' he said, rising, 'I've got time. Let's go and get a cup.'

The two men walked along the platform and into the refreshment room, where Geary bought two coffees, waving away Philip Robinson's polite request to be allowed to pay for his own. Settled at a table, facing each other, they both looked about them as if searching for a subject of conversation.

'You say you haven't just got off a train?'

'No,' Geary said. 'I've been here some time.'

Robinson hesitated; lifted his cup, drank from it; hesitated again; then said, 'How are you these days?'

'I get along,' Geary answered.

'Jennifer and I were very sorry to hear about—all that business,' said Robinson gently.

Geary shrugged. 'There was nothing else for it.'

'Yes, but . . . it's never easy. Where are you living now?'

'In an hotel,' said Geary.

Robinson was silent for a moment, as if wondering whether to leave the subject alone. The two men had never known each other well. Perhaps he had said enough; he had only brought up the matter because it seemed unfeeling to say nothing at all about Geary's troubles.

'Do you commute from town?' he asked. 'To the Institute, I mean?'

'I've given up my work at the Institute.'

Robinson's face expressed genuine surprise. 'They'll be sorry about that.'

Geary, without expression, drank from his steaming cup.

'Well, I must go,' said Robinson. He finished his coffee and stood up. 'Coming? I'm taking a taxi to South Kensington. Any use?'

'No, thanks,' said Geary, smiling. 'I'll stay here.'

Robinson looked narrowly into Geary's face for an instant. Did the man intend to hang about the station all day? Was he going to pieces? He looked calm enough, though, and reasonably healthy, well-dressed and tidy. Reassured, Robinson took his leave amid an exchange of vague expressions of willingness to see one another again.

Left alone, Geary went out to the bookstall, bought a newspaper, and, glancing at the headlines, walked slowly back into the refreshment room to finish his coffee. A West Indian, pushing a trolley, cleared away his empty cup, but Geary sat on, reading the paper, the typical image of a quiet middle-aged man who did not see why he should be hurried.

Robinson had hoped to catch a train home at about half-past four. But a garrulous chairman lengthened out a two-hour committee meeting into nearly three hours; then his taxi was caught in traffic; finally, to his great irritation, he arrived at the station in the middle of rush-hour.

Outside, the light was draining from the sky, and inside the station the electric lamps gave off a cold, inconsiderate glare. The evening was smoky and cold. From the warmth and ease of a good seat in the train, the dusky streets would look familiar and safe; the yellow squares of light would speak of home, comfort, hot tea and toast, and out in the country the darkening fields would have their own wintry peace. But the station fell somewhere in between, into a limbo. Hunched bodies, weary faces, everyone moving with the shuffling gait of one body among a thousand bodies, sealed in the loneliness of one head among a thousand heads. The trains waited with impersonal patience. Their locomotives were huge, coffin-shaped, smelling of hot oil.

Robinson, his brief-case heavy in his hand, stood in a long, coiling queue in front of the barrier that sealed off his platform. He could see the train, and longed to be comfortably inside it. But the wait to get his ticket punched was interminable. The queue was constantly broken by the hundreds of people crossing the station

from side to side, and every now and then scattered into fragments
by a long, crawling train of wagons carrying mail, and drawn by a
small red engine driven by a Post Office employee. These interrup-
tions allowed unscrupulous people to jump the queue, which they
unhesitatingly did, and Robinson began to feel that he had stood
in line for something like twenty minutes without moving forward
at all. His irritation turning into resentment, he began craning to
see over people's heads. There was his train; there was the slow,
fussing ticket-collector; there—suddenly—was Geary.

Geary was standing near the barrier. Going on the train perhaps? But no. He moved away, strolling, his grey tweed cap giving
him the air of a solid citizen out for a quiet walk on this autumn
evening. Where was he going? Forgetting his annoyance, oblivious
even of his wish to get home, Robinson watched. Geary moved
laterally along the line of ticket-barriers, then, confronted by a
scurrying knot of people, turned and went with them, exactly like
a cork being carried by the tide. An immovable queue blocked his
way; calmly, he altered course and sauntered beside them, his back
turned now to the ticket-barrier. Evidently he was in no hurry to
join the train.

He came close to Robinson, who for some reason shrank back,
fearing to be recognized. He wanted to watch Geary's behaviour,
for a few minutes at least, without having to make his presence
known. Unseeing, his face calm, Geary passed at arm's length. His
eyes moved easily about, taking in detail, as if he were on holiday,
walking round a fishing village. Robinson allowed himself, for a
moment, to cling to the notion that Geary was behaving normally;
that he had some time to wait for the train to wherever he was living
now, and all this aimless wandering was just a means of filling in
time. Robinson wanted to believe this because he longed passion-
ately to get on the train and go home. The queue happened at this
moment to advance three or four yards, and he could see the platform so clearly, and beside it the dark, motionless bulk of his train,
and beyond it he could imagine his house, the garden path wink-
ing with streaks of light from the front windows, a fire burning,
food and—oh, God—people coming to dinner. He had promised
to be home in good time. Not to leave his wife with everything to

do. And here was Geary, mooning about, presenting him with this unmistakable challenge. For Robinson was a decent man; he could not blink the fact that all was not well with Geary. And if all was not well, then Geary must be helped. He must not be left in this comfortless twilight, alone, unidentified, among strangers.

Robinson left the queue. At once the people behind him moved firmly up and closed the gap. He could never come back now. The tiny Rubicon was crossed. He would telephone his wife, then go and look after Geary, and the train would go out without him.

What drove him was the knowledge, confirmed by a fresh view of Geary's grey tweed cap moving about among the crowd, that Geary was not waiting for a train, or keeping a rendezvous, or searching for the information office, or the barber's shop; that he was walking about the station: just that, and nothing more: *walking about the station*.

Surveying the row of motionless backs and profiles, Robinson waited for a telephone. His train would be gone in nine minutes; in eight, in seven, in six, in five. A door opened, a telephone beckoned. The coins ready in his hand, he sprang into the box.

'Hello?'

'Hello?'

'Jennifer, this is me. Philip.'

'Yes. What's wrong? You're coming home, aren't you? I hope to *goodness* you won't choose this evening to be—'

'Listen, darling. This is important. I've just seen Arthur Geary and he's in a bad way.'

'What kind of bad way is he in? Anyway, you can talk about it on the train, can't you?'

'He's not taking the train.'

'Well, that's too bad, isn't it? (Julian, leave that alone. Go and tell Julian to leave that alone, quickly!) Look, Philip, never mind about Arthur Geary. Just come home.'

'But let me tell you, darling. He seems to have had some sort of nervous breakdown. He's wandering about the station. I saw him this morning and he must have been here all day.'

'How d'you know he's been there all day? (Julian! *Leave that alone!!!*) Did he say so?'

'Well, not exactly.'

'What d'you mean, not exactly? Aren't you catching the six o'clock? What's going on?'

'I haven't spoken to him this evening. I've only *seen* him. As a matter of fact, I'm watching him now.'

'You haven't spoken to him, but you know he's spent all day at the station because you saw him there this morning and he's there now? Well, so are you, aren't you?'

'Look Jennifer, let me get one thing straight. I'm ringing you because I'm not going to get on the six o'clock.'

'Oh, *no*! You *can't* have forgotten that Keith and Alice are—'

'No, I haven't forgotten, but if I take the next train I can be home by half-past eight—'

'*Half-past* EIGHT?'

'I must see that he gets to a doctor or something. Or at least talk to him and find out what it's—'

'Philip, for God's sake, if you run now you'll catch the six o'clock and I *need* you, don't you understand?'

'Arthur Geary—'

'You're married to me, not Arthur Geary,' his wife hissed between clenched teeth. 'You've got an obligation to me and to the home we make together. You've gone through your *whole life* without bothering about Arthur Geary—and now, just because I ask you . . .'

Trembling, Robinson put down the receiver. To ring off. In American, to hang up. He had rung off, hung up, on his wife to whom he had been married nineteen years. Which sounded more offensive? I hung up on her. I rang off on her. He pushed the door of the telephone booth and walked out in search of Geary.

The grey cap was standing still near the bookstall. Robinson heard his train hoot derisively just before moving off. He touched Geary's shoulder.

'Hello,' he said nervously.

'We meet again,' said Geary easily. He stood, apparently relaxed, among milling bodies.

'I've missed my train,' said Robinson. 'Damned annoying, as we've got people coming to dinner. My wife'll be . . .' he sweated. 'Let's go and have a beer, if you're waiting too.'

As he said the last words Robinson allowed his eyebrows to wander slightly upwards, conveying a delicate hint of the interrogative. He prided himself on the subtlety of this hint. Without seeming to give the conversation an unduly personal turn it gave Geary the perfect opportunity to explain what he was doing, still on the station after all these hours. But Geary seemed unaware that there was anything to explain.

'The bars are a bit crowded,' he said, 'but I expect we'll get something. The one over there's best, I think.'

He pointed to a corner of the foyer. A sign said LICENSED BUFFET. The two men began to make their way across to it. Robinson, as he pushed and dodged, felt rage beginning to rise in his breast. If he had put himself into an exceedingly unpleasant position for the sake of helping Geary, it was surely up to Geary to let himself be helped.

The buffet was hot and steamy. One end of the bar was for tea and coffee, the other was 'licensed'. The licensed end was heavily jammed with customers. Men snatched glasses and gulped, as if they had trains leaving in a few minutes, or nursed glasses and stared morosely round, as if they had missed their trains and saw a desert of time ahead. The two middle-aged barmaids worked stolidly, not hurrying but never pausing. Robinson and Geary both chose to drink bottled beer. They waited in silence to be served, then moved painfully away from the crowded bar and found a bench in a corner where, jammed together, they could at least talk.

'Cheers,' said Robinson.

'Cheers.'

Robinson drank, then looked Geary straight in the eye. 'I say, you mustn't think me interfering, but is everything all right?'

'How d'you mean exactly?'

'Well,' said Robinson, controlling himself, 'I mean are you all right?'

Geary looked meditative. 'Don't I seem all right?'

'Well, I don't mind telling you I missed my train on purpose because I felt concerned about you.'

'Very good of you, Philip. I appreciate it.'

'Now look here,' said Robinson, squaring his shoulders, 'it

seems to me we're in danger of getting bogged down in—in evasions.'

'That's a hard word,' said Geary, smiling.

'Would you mind telling me,' Robinson went on determinedly, 'how long you've been on this station?'

'Nine days,' said Geary.

There was a pause. Then Robinson said, 'Nine *days*?'

To his shame, he felt a surge of something that was unmistakably relief. So Geary *was* mad! So Jennifer would have to forgive him for missing the dinner-party!

'But why, why?' he said, speaking vehemently to drown that nasty little spark of gladness.

'It suits me.'

'But . . .' Robinson gestured helplessly. 'You don't mean that you've spent your entire time on the station for *nine days*?'

'No,' said Geary. 'I sleep in the hotel at night. I go to bed at about eleven o'clock. In the mornings I don't hurry: it's half-past nine before I get down here.'

'You sleep in what hotel?'

'The station hotel,' said Geary.

'Look, let me get this straight,' said Robinson. 'You spend your nights in the station hotel and your days walking about on the platforms?'

'Sometimes walking, sometimes just sitting. And I have my meals in the different refreshment rooms. I'm getting to be quite an authority on them.'

'May I ask what the purpose is?'

'I could talk about it,' said Geary, 'but with all due respect to you, Philip, I don't see why I should.'

'Well, let me just ask this,' said Robinson. 'Is it part of a survey or something? I mean, is there some purpose behind it?'

'If you mean did somebody ask me to do it, no. It's a purely personal decision.'

'And it isn't for the sake of gathering information or any-thing?'

'Not in the sense you probably mean.'

'All right,' said Robinson. He stood up. 'If you want to spend

your time here, it's your affair. But I suppose you can understand
how it looks from the outside.'

'How does it look?'

'It looks,' said Robinson bitterly, 'as if you've had some sort
of breakdown that's left you incapable of behaving in a rational
manner.'

'Behaving in a rational manner,' said Geary. 'I suppose you
attach some clear meaning to those words, Philip. Or do you just
mean behaving like everybody else?'

'Don't try to tangle the discussion any further, please, Arthur.
You know quite well what I mean.'

'If every large railway station had a hundred people living on it
permanently, and you'd always been used to the idea, it wouldn't
seem irrational at all,' said Geary. 'You accept far more arbitrary
things, every day of your life.'

Robinson stood up abruptly. His evening was in ruins, his
domestic peace would probably not be recoverable for weeks if
not months, and here was Geary, the man he had done all this to
help, placidly denying that he needed any help. He looked down at
Geary, whose grey tweed cap, seen from above, radiated an infuri-
ating calm.

'All right, Arthur,' he said. 'I missed my train because I was
worried about you, but it seems you think I was just wasting my
time.'

'Well, I appreciate it very much,' said Geary, 'and it's always a
pleasure to talk to you. I'm sorry you missed your train.'

'Do you know what I find the most frightening thing of all?' said
Robinson, bending down. 'Your *calm*.'

Geary picked up his glass and drank a little. 'I don't see why I
shouldn't be calm. You asked me how long I'd been on the station
and I thought it was better to tell you than beat about the bush.
After all, I know you as a sensible and well-disposed man. You
won't immediately try to get me put into a padded cell because
I'm doing something that isn't always done by everybody.'

'Well, since we talk of padded cells,' said Robinson, still driven
by his anger, 'I might as well say what's in my mind. If you stay
here you'll go mad. The crowds, the discomfort, the sense of

homelessness, will unhinge you. Go on, laugh at me, but you'll be raving mad inside three months.'

'Would you care to make a bet on that?' Geary asked, smiling.

'With pleasure,' said Robinson. 'But it'll be difficult to collect the money from you if you're certified insane.'

The word had slipped out. It might as well be left lying there, in full view. Both men were silent for a moment, then Geary said, 'That's what you really think, isn't it?'

'I think,' said Robinson slowly, 'that you've been under great emotional strain and you must be very exhausted and you probably aren't in a position to judge what's best for you.'

'In other words, mentally ill,' said Geary. There was another pause and then he asked, 'Did you ever know a man called Geoffrey Winters?'

'The name seems to ring a bell. Would I have known him?'

'He was a micro-biologist,' said Geary.

'What about him?'

'Geoffrey was the loneliest man I ever knew. He said he could find absolutely no way of getting into contact with humanity as a whole. He was attached to a few individuals, chiefly I think to his wife and to me, but that wasn't enough. He felt as if he spent about eighteen hours utterly beyond human reach, out on some planet that hadn't a single other inhabitant.'

'What happened to him?'

'He killed himself,' said Geary flatly.

Robinson leaned over Geary.

After a pause Robinson asked, 'Why are you telling me this?'

'Well,' said Geary, 'suppose Geoffrey had found a way of overcoming his loneliness, even if it was a bit eccentric. Wouldn't it be better to let him go ahead with it, rather than force him back to what you call rationality and make him so unbearably lonely that he poisoned himself one morning in his own kitchen?'

Robinson still leaned over Geary, staring down into his face. 'Is that what you're trying to tell me? That you'll commit suicide if you're not allowed to stay here?'

'Of course not,' said Geary. He laughed with what seemed to be genuine amusement. 'I never said anything about myself and

I won't have you putting extravagant nonsense into my mouth. I was just bringing to your attention a case in which rational behaviour, as you call it, doesn't seem to have helped much.'

Robinson straightened up. 'I think I'll go,' he said. 'You're telling me, in pretty unmistakable terms, to mind my own business. And at the same time you're quite gratuitously bringing up the case of some friend of yours who committed suicide because he was lonely. That's the kind of thing your mind's running on, and yet you claim that you're all right.'

'I never said that,' said Geary. 'I don't think anybody's all right. You're putting words into my mouth again.'

'All right, I'll go,' said Robinson.

'Please yourself, Philip,' said Geary, 'but your train isn't for some time. Why not sit down and have another beer? The place isn't so crowded now and we can have a comfortable talk.'

'What about?' asked Robinson. 'Suicide?'

He strode out on to the platform, and without hesitation kept moving until he had left the station behind and was walking down a series of mean, crumbling streets. Anything to get away from this impasse. He would go back to the station five minutes before his train time, and not before. He did not want to meet Geary again. He felt full of pity, bewilderment, annoyance, anxiety, and—suddenly stronger than any of them—fatigue. It had been a long day.

Back in the refreshment room Geary ordered a glass of stout and calmly unfolded the evening paper.

As Geary was drinking his stout in the refreshment room, his wife, sixty-five miles away, was talking on the telephone.

Elizabeth Geary had never been pretty. As a girl, she was what people called handsome, and this handsomeness was scarcely impaired at forty. Her face was almost entirely free of wrinkles and the plumpness of her hips only gave her a pleasing maturity in keeping with her air of unruffled authority. She kept a neat engagement book, three days to a page, beside the telephone, and as she talked she glanced down at it, not because she was making an engagement but simply from force of habit.

'Well, thank you, I'm coping,' she said. 'In fact from that point of view, keeping everything going and the children cared for, the only *real* difference is that I shall have to stop doing so much work for nothing. I've told the Ministry I shall need a salaried post and they've promised to find me one in the New Year by the latest. So *that's* all right.'

'I think you're very brave,' said the meaningless woman at the other end of the line, who was telephoning about some committee business. Mrs. Geary was on a number of committees. 'I just don't know how I should manage.'

'You'd manage because you'd have to manage, my dear,' said Mrs. Geary. 'And anyway, there's one blessing: even in this day and age it doesn't happen very often. Most husbands stay with their wives. It's only the occasional one like Arthur who suddenly takes it into his head that he wants to go off and live by himself.'

The woman at the other end was very curious to know whether Arthur Geary had in fact gone off with a girl, so she jumped eagerly on the words 'by himself' and set herself to test their genuineness.

'How ever is he managing? That's what I don't understand,' she said.

'I have no information on that point,' said Elizabeth Geary, glancing down at her engagement book. 'Till my solicitor chooses to communicate with me I don't even know where Arthur's living. He's done what they call "the decent thing" about money, leaving me and the children with the bulk of what was available, and—' her face took on a brave look—'for the moment that's all I'm allowing myself to think about.'

'Yes, of course, I quite understand,' said her interlocutor, her mind busy with the question of whether this constituted proof that Arthur Geary had gone off with a mistress who had some money in the bank. It was always the quiet ones, she thought. 'Well, I'll get those figures in time for Tuesday afternoon, Elizabeth, and meanwhile perhaps you could go and see the probation people and find out what they intend to do about it.' It will do you good, her voice said, to have some errands to run, you poor manless darling.

'I shall have their account of it by Tuesday,' said Mrs. Geary. A door opened and she turned her head. Her daughter Angela, aged fifteen, was making one of her entrances. 'I must go now, I'm afraid, unless there's anything else you—'

The other woman, snubbed, hastened to say that there was nothing more, and took herself off the line. Replacing the receiver with a firm, precise movement, Mrs. Geary turned to give her full attention to her daughter.

'Mummy,' said Angela, 'have you thought about it yet?'

Mrs. Geary sighed. Angela had no sooner been left (to all intents and purposes) fatherless than she had begun to pester her mother to move to London. 'After all, we only stayed in this awful backward place because Daddy was working at the Institute. There's no reason at all, now, why we shouldn't live like human beings.'

'And do human beings only live in London?' Mrs. Geary had asked. She had intended to load her voice with irony, but the irony, she realized, came through only faintly. At bottom, she herself thought it a mistake not to live in the capital city of the nation you happened to belong to. It gave more scope, and scope was something she approved of. Hence her failure to bury Angela's question under a snowfall of large, tolerant irony.

'Angela, darling,' she now said firmly, 'you know quite well it's far too early to make decisions of that kind. Everything's still unsettled. I've nothing against moving to London, in principle, but we must know our circumstances first. If your father and I are going to be divorced,' she brought out the word in a light, matter-of-fact tone, just a fact to be faced and nothing more, 'there will have to be a money settlement. And just how much we can expect I don't know, especially now that I hear your father has resigned from the Institute.'

'Mummy,' said Angela, twisting her head round to try to look at her own spine, 'why did Daddy move out?'

'I've told you, darling, I don't know. Men sometimes do strange things when they get to that age. Forty-five,' Mrs. Geary added, wishing to be precise.

Angela tried to look over the other shoulder. She was anxious to see how her dress fitted at the back. 'But didn't he say *anything*? I mean, did he just get up one evening and walk out without a *word*?'

'Darling, there's a perfectly good full-length mirror in your bedroom. You needn't get a slipped disc or something. He said he was lonely.'

'*Lonely?*' Angela straightened up and looked at her mother. 'With all of us about all the time?'

'That's what he said.'

'But how does it make him less lonely to go off and be by himself?'

'I don't know, darling. It's as mysterious to me as it is to you.'

A thought struck Angela. 'Mummy, *is* he by himself?'

'As far as I know, darling,' said Mrs. Geary with admirable self-possession.

'But you *don't* know, do you? I bet it'll turn out that he's going to get married again. Probably to somebody about my age. That's what they usually do, isn't it? Men. . . . I bet he'll be embarrassed when he has to introduce me to her. But of course he'll have spent money on her and she'll be dressed *marvellously* and that'll give her confidence. . . . If I could only have *one new skirt* . . . you've been putting me off and putting me off and it's *years* since I—'

'Angela, my love,' said Mrs. Geary, getting up from her chair, 'you've been pestering me to buy you a leather skirt, costing as much as three or four ordinary skirts put together, and if it's going to get mixed up in your mind with all sorts of unhealthy fantasies about your father marrying a fifteen-year-old girl and then the two of you having a rivalry for his affections, all I can say is, it's time you went to bed. You need plenty of rest at your age.'

Upstairs, David lay on his back in bed with the sheet drawn tightly up to his chin. Something had woken him and now he could not go to sleep again. He decided to think. There was no time to think except in the night; in the daytime it was hurry to get up, hurry to get ready, hurry to go to school, waste all day messing about in school, come home, do homework, go to bed. David hated his life; his chief comfort was that it would not always be like this. His father had told him so. Once, years and years ago, when he was about seven or even *six*, his father had noticed that he was unhappy and taken him on his knee and talked to him. 'Life changes, you know,' he had said. 'Every few years it alters and gets quite different. No unhappiness lasts for ever. So all you have to do is go forward. Remember that, won't you?' David had said Yes and he had remembered it.

Lying in the soft glow of the night-light, he thought briefly about his father, but soon drifted into thinking about ducks. He often went to feed the ducks on the circular pond in the park. The pond was close to the river and sometimes the ducks went to swim in the river for a change, but they always came back to the pond. When he was very young, people had taken him to feed the ducks, but now he went by himself. He kept a bag in the kitchen and collected crusts and stray pieces of bread and cake; he was in command of the whole operation.

The ducks bobbed like toy boats. Actually some were ducks and some were drakes. He knew about that. But you never seemed to see them doing it. Perhaps they did it at night, like human beings. The important thing about the drakes was their lovely colouring that changed with the light as they moved about. Oily colours on the flat muddy water. Stiff bare reeds in the winter.

Why was it so much fun to feed the ducks? They fought and dashed for the bread as he threw it to them. Sometimes he would decide that a certain one was not getting enough; the quicker or fiercer ducks were taking the bread from under its nose. Then he would begin to aim all his bread at that one bird. If it kept missing he would cunningly throw several pieces of bread to make it move in a direction of its own, away from the others where it would have more chance. By tossing bread to one side of the duck you could make it go to that side. It was like moving one piece on a chess-board. Or like God. God could take one person and move him this way with an illness or that way with a happiness. When you moved one duck from among the others you did it to be kind. But you could do it to be unkind if you liked. You could move one duck all over the pond and always throw the pieces of bread a little too far ahead so that it never got anything to eat, just kept on moving and moving. God could do that if he liked. But ducks didn't know how to pray. If they could pray what would they say?

He was like God but he would be kind. The ducks would get

to know him and they would realize that when David threw them bread it was so that they should have it to eat, and not just to move them about. And so in one small spot of the universe, one round pond with stiff reeds, kindness and justice would rule.

He would tell his father that. He would like that idea. If he ever saw him again, he would tell him: the duck-pond is a happy place, because of me. Then his father would smile.

'I don't want anything to eat, thanks, darling,' Philip Robinson said to his wife. 'I thought it would be simpler for you to go ahead and have dinner without me, so I had something on the train.'

'I've kept yours warm,' she said coldly and furiously. Obviously it was only the presence of the two visitors, Keith and Alice Doulton, that stopped her from setting about him with the full armoury of feminine weapons.

'Do forgive me,' said Robinson, smiling, to his guests. 'I expect Jennifer told you how I came to be delayed.'

'Something about Arthur Geary,' said Keith Doulton, a short, calm man who smoked a short, calm pipe.

'I do hope he's all right now,' said Alice Doulton, doing her bit to cover up the domestic tension. Her lack of genuine interest in Arthur Geary showed through as plainly as something printed on the back of a flimsy sheet of paper. 'Did you manage to calm him down before you left?'

'Oh, that wasn't necessary,' said Robinson, pouring himself a large whisky. He avoided his wife's eyes. 'He was quite calm all along.'

'But I thought he was refusing to leave the station,' she persisted. 'We had visions of a scene, with him struggling with policemen.'

'Nobody's tried to make him leave the station yet,' said Robinson, 'if only because nobody knows he's spending all his time there.'

'Nobody except you,' said his wife with quiet venom.

'Well, it's a free country,' said Doulton judicially.

'Madness is nothing to do with freedom, Keith,' said Robinson.

The whisky had given him back his courage and he spoke shortly and positively.

'Madness?' Doulton's eyes widened. 'You put it as strongly as that?'

'I thought you said he was quite calm,' said Alice Doulton.

'It all depends on what kind of madness Philip has in mind,' said her husband. 'Obviously some forms of mental disorder leave one very calm, outwardly.'

'You mean he's got delusions or something?' asked Alice Doulton. 'If you ask me, it's much more likely that he's telling a trumped-up story to pull the wool over Philip's eyes.'

How fitting, Robinson reflected, that such a woman should express herself entirely in shopworn clichés. Leaning back in his chair, he narrowed his eyes slightly and looked at his guests, finding a kind of relish in the strength and purity of his dislike for them. Mrs. Doulton was a thin, birdlike, beaky woman of the type that is described in youth as 'petite' and 'vivacious'. Her smallness accentuated her husband's, so that the pair of them looked like the inhabitants of a doll's house, out on an excursion. Sitting up stiffly, like toys, they seemed prepared to discuss Geary as they would have discussed any story they chanced on in a newspaper.

Jennifer Robinson, a tall, cool woman whose expression never wandered far from the expressionless even when she was delighted or enraged, now addressed Alice Doulton. 'Alice, why should Arthur Geary want to deceive anyone?'

'Well, of course, you know,' Mrs. Doulton said with relish, 'that he's abandoned his wife and children.'

'They've split up, certainly,' said Robinson. 'I think we all know that.'

'Well, then,' said Alice Doulton. 'There'll be a divorce case, and there'll be detectives and the Queen's Proctor and all sorts of investigations.' It was obvious from the sparkle in her eyes that she loved to speak of such matters. 'So naturally when Arthur Geary sees anyone he knows on Paddington Station, he covers his tracks at once.'

Robinson could not be bothered to answer, and once again it was Jennifer Robinson who took up the conversation. 'Have you ever met his wife? I was introduced to her once but I can't remember her name.'

'Elizabeth,' said Mrs. Doulton promptly. 'I never met her, but I remember somebody telling me how nice she was and what a wonderful home she made for them all. I remember the person's exact words. "Elizabeth Geary is the best-organized woman I know".'

'A doubtful compliment,' said Doulton, smiling.

'Oh, I know how your mind works,' said his wife. 'Any woman who has a sense of responsibility to her husband and family is a python or something who's trying to strangle them all, that's what you think, isn't it?'

'Men think a house runs itself,' said Jennifer Robinson. 'They go out of the place in the morning and from then on they think it runs itself while we sit under the hair-drier and read magazines.'

The two women, united in their sense of oppression, looked sternly at their husbands.

'To get back to Arthur Geary,' said Doulton. Everybody expected him to continue, but he was lighting his pipe, and they had to wait while he sucked the flame once, twice, three times into the blackened bowl. Then he waved out the match and resumed. 'Personally I discount Alice's theory. He wouldn't tell an untruth that was so easy to verify. If he's living on the station, then he's staying either at the station hotel or at another one very close by, and an investigator could check the whole lot in half an hour.'

'What have investigators got to do with it?' asked Robinson, his patience cracking. 'If all the detectives in the world got together they wouldn't make a scrap of difference. Arthur Geary is a man in trouble, it's as simple as that. I don't know him very well and I can't attempt to say what's the matter with him, but somehow or other life has got on top of him and destroyed his capacity for dealing with his experience.'

'So he goes and lives on the station,' Mrs. Doulton mocked. 'Is he fixated on trains or something?'

'I wonder how he's managing the financial side of things,' said Doulton. 'I mean, that would give some idea of whether he's got any grip on reality.'

'Why would it?' said Robinson. 'Some people are obsession-
ally efficient about money and at the same time they live in pure
fantasy.'

'Still,' said Doulton, puffing, 'if he's left his wife with adequate
funds, it does mean that his sense of responsibility's in working
order.'

'It *doesn't*,' said Alice Doulton. 'To go off and leave her to carry
the whole thing by herself—that's irresponsible whichever way
you look at it. The money isn't everything, as you seem to think,
Keith.'

Robinson poured himself another drink, ignoring his wife's
raised eyebrows. He was beginning to feel that they would certify
him as insane next. 'Look,' he said, 'we're just talking round the
subject—'

'Julian!' said Mrs. Robinson sharply, 'how long have you been
there?'

All looked towards the door, which was now seen to be ajar.
A shock-headed, half-grown child, in pyjamas and with bare feet,
was dimly visible, standing motionless in the hall, some six feet
from the door.

'Come in here, Julian,' commanded Mrs. Robinson.

The figure slowly approached and looked in at them, without
entering.

'Why aren't you in bed?' Mrs. Robinson demanded.

'I was hungry. I came down to get a biscuit.'

'Well, have you got one?'

Julian hesitantly opened his right hand and showed the remaining half of a wholemeal biscuit clutched in the palm.

'Off you go now. Good-night,' said his father gently.

'Good-night. Dad?'

'Yes?'

'Will you come and tuck me up?'

'You're too big for that now,' Mrs. Robinson intervened.

'But my bed's all slipped to one side.'

'I'll see to it,' said Robinson, standing up. He was already so
deep in his wife's disapproval that he could hardly make things
worse by disobeying her again; he knew that she disliked these

occasional regressions into babyhood on the part of nine-year-old
Julian. But he understood how Julian felt. The world was a cold,
grey place and anyone might feel the need to be tucked into bed
and kissed. As he followed Julian upstairs, the sight of the boy's
fragile body suddenly touched a spring of pity in this prosaic
man's heart. He thought of Arthur Geary, sitting on a bench in the
hooded twilight of the station: alone, drifting rudderless on the
cold sea of time, and suddenly finding himself compelled to hang
on desperately to the impersonal, unwelcoming spar of rock that
was the station. Arthur Geary had once been nine years old like
Julian. Panic gripped Robinson as he thought of Julian growing
up in the world that had reduced Geary, a solid and gifted man,
to such a state. . . . He kissed the boy, tucked him up with great
care (the bed, he found, was only slightly disarranged), then went
downstairs with an ice-cold determination in his heart.

'I know what we ought to do,' he announced, walking into the
living-room.

'Oh, damn Arthur Geary,' said his wife. 'We'd started to talk
about something else and you've no idea how pleasant it was.'

He stared at her. 'You can go on talking about something else.
I'm going to ring up Maurice Blakeney.'

'Maurice Blakeney?' Doulton puckered his forehead. 'The
Grayson man?'

The local mental hospital, whose full name was 'The Charles
Grayson Hospital and Clinic', was known to everyone simply as
'the Grayson'.

'He takes private patients too,' said Robinson. He finished
his whisky without sitting down. 'Jennifer and I know him
slightly.'

'And you're going to ring him now and tell him about Arthur
Geary?' his wife asked incredulously.

'If he's in. If not, I'll ring tomorrow morning. I don't think
there's any time to lose.'

'You mean Arthur Geary might throw himself off the platform
under a train or something?'

'What Arthur Geary might or might not do,' said Robinson,
feeling that if he did not assert himself now his wife would rule

him for ever, 'is not my concern. All I know is that he's ill and his case should be brought to the notice of a man who understands illnesses of that kind.'

'Be careful,' said Doulton. 'You might find yourself landed with the bill.' He smiled cautiously round the stem of his pipe.

'I'd rather be landed with the bill,' said Robinson, 'than with the feeling that I stood by and did nothing to help him.'

Going out into the hall, where the telephone was kept, he put on his glasses and dialled Dr. Blakeney's number.

At the station hotel, Geary had a room with a private bath. He had hesitated over this at first, but after a day or two he had decided that a certain degree of comfort, a pleasant corner to retire to at night, did not unduly interfere with his involvement in the life of the station.

It was eleven o'clock on the evening of the day after his meeting with Robinson. He had just finished having a bath, and was drying himself. His pyjamas were ready to put on; he had intended to go to bed early. But now, as he towelled his back, Geary suddenly felt that to go to bed so soon would be a defeat. He had spoken to no one that day. Early in the morning, scanning one of the book-stalls, he had discovered an interesting book by a man who had once been a colleague of his at the Institute. It was popularization, but with some original ideas of the author's own, and Geary had always meant to read it. He had bought it, begun it there and then, over breakfast, and devoted the whole day to reading the book and thinking about it. As a result, the time had passed quickly and hap-pily; but now, with his solitary bed waiting for him, he felt the need of people. He decided to go down to the refreshment room and have a nightcap.

He began putting on his clothes. A nightcap? Tea or coffee would keep him awake, and the law of England forbade a comforting alcoholic drink. Hot milk? Yes, and take his pocket-flask down and put a little whisky in it. Without, of course, letting them see him do it, because of the law of England. He smiled slightly, knotting his tie. A hot milk, among human beings, with a little whisky and perhaps a last look at his ex-colleague's book. There were some passages he wanted to go over again, slowly. Then he would have the book lodged securely in his mind, available for meditation and analysis.

Geary put his hip-flask, newly filled from an excellent bottle of Scotch, into his coat pocket. Then, relaxed and happy, he took the lift down and walked out on to the station. There were still plenty of people about. Only after midnight did the platforms become rather empty. But he was usually in bed then.

He pushed open the door of the nearest refreshment room. There were three on the station, and this, the least pleasant, was also the only one that stayed open late. It was difficult not to conclude that the station authorities had decided, perhaps unconsciously, that to provide a service for belated travellers was already enough; to let them have it in one of the more spacious and cheerful rooms might be too much. This one, which Geary had come to know well, was divided into two. After taking your tray and moving along a railed-in space beside the counter to be served, you could either sit down in the same room or pass through an archway into another room. The arrangement was no doubt a relic of the time when this part of the station buildings had been used for something else. It had the advantage that the second room was not visible from behind the counter, so that any malpractice, such as pouring a little whisky into a glass of hot milk after eleven o'clock, remained undetected by the personnel. For this and kindred reasons, the further room attracted the kind of character who wished to remain unobtrusive. Men who had drunk too much went there to sleep it off with their heads on the tables. Tramps changed their socks, and adolescents bought and sold packets of heroin, in the shadow under its tables.

Geary took his hot milk, went into the further room, and sat looking about him. He was trying to decide what exactly constituted its appalling hideousness. It was difficult to single anything out, since every object the eye encountered was an ugly shape or an ugly colour or both. In the whole room there was nothing to raise the spirits of a human being, and since the place was necessarily frequented by many people who were tired or anxious, it

was remarkable (Geary reflected) that it did not cause a greater
number of immediate suicides.

He himself felt quite cheerful. Sitting back, he took stock of
the room and decided that the most offensive objects were a row
of stools running down its further side. These stools, screwed into
the floor, consisted of polished metal stalks topped by flat revolving seats in some form of *ersatz* leather. As Geary contemplated
the stools, they seemed to yield up the whole secret of the modern
mass society. You can't move the stools about the room, they are
fixed in their exact equidistance, but you can revolve them. Limited
freedom! Naught for your comfort, all for your convenience! The
metal mushroom-stalks seemed to grin at him like artificial teeth
in a sarcastic mouth.

Slowly, Geary felt in his pocket for the flask of whisky. The steam
rose from his hot milk as he unscrewed the top and measured out
two exact capfuls. He had always enjoyed a nightcap of whisky;
now it was important to see that the habit did not get hold of him.
He must avoid any temptation to step up the quantity.

He poured, replaced the cap, and was just raising the glass to his
lips when he became aware that a voice was addressing him.

'That's a great friend to a man on a cold night and no mistake.'

Geary turned his head. The old Irishman had already been cultivating this particular friendship in no half-hearted fashion. His
pendulous nose was vermilion, his eyes yellow and half-closed. But
he managed a cheerful smile as he limped over to join Geary at his
table.

'Well and all, it's a God-forsaken country,' he remarked, deftly
plucking the flask from Geary's hand, 'where a man can't get a
drop of the right stuff when he feels weary and down at heart.' He
was raising the flask to his lips when Geary hastily caught his wrist.

'Pour yourself some out, by all means,' he said, 'but don't drink
out of the bottle.'

The Irishman laughed tolerantly. 'Afraid I'll take too much at
one time, eh? Well, it's kind of yez to offer it and I appreciate it.
God be with Connemara where they drink it out of buckets.' He
picked up a cup, left on the table by some departed patron and
sniffed it. 'H'm. Tea. All right. If it had been coffee, I'd have looked

for another one. But tea never got in the way of a good ball of malt.' He splashed whisky into the cup to half its depth. 'Here's to your kind heart. An Englishman, but with a true brotherly feeling to a fellow-creature. A decent skin ye are, I can see that. God be with Connemara. That's where I come from and I wish I was there this minute.'

'So do I,' said Geary.

'Ah, that's like your kind heart. You don't meet many right-thinking men these days. God be with the days that have gone. This country's too many darkies in it now. A white man can't find work, not even if he's ready to get down on all fours, like a horse.'

He poured out more whisky. Geary, closing his book, looked round for escape. His eyes encountered those of a powerfully built young man, in stained working clothes and heavy boots, who was glaring suspiciously at him from one of the neighbouring stools.

'Darkies everywhere,' said the Connemara man. 'But not in the rough jobs. If a white man wants work to do today, he's to creep under the ground like a mole. I was workin' today. They had me down in a hole under the street there, pushing wires down a long tube, and the water running down me like a washboard.'

'Very unpleasant,' said Geary.

'Not a darkie in sight,' said the old man. 'They melted away fast when they didn't like the look of the job. Sixty-seven years old, I am. I should be telling them what to do, instead of going down a hole with water pouring over me the way it would break your soft heart to see it. My good old mother if she could see me would be after walking up out of the ground. I didn't think to go under the soil till they put me in my grave. That won't be long now, God be with the time. And all the fault of those heathen black niggers.'

'I don't quite understand how it was their fault,' said Geary.

'Their fault?' The old man's face twisted with rage. 'Their fault that a white man old enough to be their father was crouching down like a beast with the water running down his back? They were taking cocaine. I saw them sniffing it up. No Christian man would take drugs, answer me *that* now.' He slumped forward across the table, squinting up at Geary. 'Tell me the whys and wherefores of *that*, mister, if you can. I saw them sniffing it up into their black noses, the animals.'

'Have some more whisky,' said Geary. He had decided that it would be better to see his flask emptied than to endure the man's company any longer, and he saw no prospect of getting away until the whisky was gone.

He poured out most of what remained, but the Connemara man had reached the aggressive phase of drunkenness. He tossed it down and sat, breathing fire, his aggrieved eye fastened on Geary's. 'Old enough to be their father, and when I straightened my back and came out of the hole the foreman told me I had the sack. I asked him why and he said for knocking off when 'twasn't knocking-off time. And those black heathen going behind the shed to sniff up cocaine. They must have bribed him. He never said nothing about sacking *them*.'

'Look,' said Geary gently, 'I can see you've had a bad day and you've got a real grievance. Why don't you go home now and get some sleep? Then tomorrow—'

'Sleep!' shouted the Connemara citizen. 'Don't be after mocking me now. I'm old enough to be your father. You know I've got no home to go to. It's divil the place to sleep I've got. You're mocking me, you English git.' He began to weep loudly.

'No, I'm not,' said Geary desperately. He saw, out of the corner of his eye, that the strong young workman had got down from his stool and was coming over towards them. 'I didn't know you had no home,' he said to the weeping old man. 'How was I to?'

'Stop taking the mickey out of him,' said the young man in a low, murderous voice, bending down to Geary's ear. His accent was identical with the old man's.

'That's right, Paddy,' sobbed the old man. 'First the darkies and then him, making a mock of me. It's been a terrible day surely.' He whimpered quietly into his cup.

'Step outside, mister. We'll see who's making a mock,' said the young Irishman. Geary, looking up at him, had a vivid impression of thick, corded veins in his neck, swelling with rage.

'I wasn't—' he began.

'Come outside or have it in here, it don't make no difference to me,' the young Irishman breathed. He turned his head rapidly to right and left, obviously weighing up the risk of interruption. It was small. There were only two other men there, and an old woman asleep with her head on a table in the corner. The two men, wispy figures in long overcoats, rapidly put down their cups and disappeared. Geary watched them go. His brain was racing for a solution of the problem, but nothing suggested itself.

It was all over quite quickly. The young Irishman, remarking in an almost conversational tone, 'You're a puking English bastard,' swung his fist into Geary's face, causing a dark torrent of blood to drench Geary's shirt-front and jacket. Geary slipped sideways from his chair, clutching at his face. As he did so, the Irishman swung his boot once, twice, a third time. Each time the boot thudded in, Geary gave a loud, non-human grunt. The young Irishman walked calmly to the door, out, and was lost in the shadow of the station. The old man got to his feet, cast a confused, frightened glance at Geary's inert form, and stumbled after him. 'Paddy!' he could be heard calling plaintively. 'Paddy! Would you take me with ye?' His voice soon died away.

The old woman in the corner woke up, lifted her head from her crossed arms and saw Geary. He was leaning on one elbow, feebly waving one arm like a crushed insect. 'My Gawd,' the old woman squawked. 'There's murder here, murder!' The voices in the other room became stilled. 'Murder!' she shouted again. 'Let me out of here! I never saw what happened! I was asleep!'

Several people peered round the doorway. When they saw Geary bleeding on the floor, they hesitated a moment, then came forward and picked him up. Someone telephoned for a doctor. A policeman was brought in from the street outside. Geary was made as comfortable as possible. He was muttering broken sentences in a low voice, and blood continued to splash from his nose. His breathing was shallow. It seemed to him, and to everyone present, a long time before the ambulance came.

It was not far to the hospital. The casualty doctor on duty treated Geary immediately. With his face cleaned, his bleeding staunched, his cracked ribs encased in plaster, he felt more cheerful and managed to drink a cup of tea. His nose, for some reason, was not broken. A young nurse, her soft inexperience well shielded by the starch of her apron and cuffs, the dazzle of her white cap, came to ask for his particulars.

'They won't let you go home tonight,' she said. 'D'you want to telephone home?'

'No, thank you,' said Geary. 'But I'd better tell my hotel not to let my room go.'

'We can do that for you,' she said. 'What hotel is it?'

He named the station hotel. 'Does the doctor say when I can go home?' he asked.

'Tomorrow, I expect. We only need to keep an eye on you for tonight. You're not in any danger. But you've got a bit of shock, I expect, being set on like that.' She gave him a look of sympathy and moved off on her duties.

Geary lay back. Shock? Did he feel shock? Cautiously, he tested his mind, feeling it inch by inch to see if anything was broken or badly bruised. He felt perfectly calm. Had they injected a sedative into him? He could not remember. At any rate, he felt only one thing: a wish to get back as soon as possible to the station. The hospital was all right; he could stand it for one night. He was in a large ward, and all round him were beds occupied by sleeping forms; the long, high room was drowned in a thick silence like a treacherous sea in which wicked sharks of pain were swimming just below the surface, their fins poking out. Now and again someone cried out, sharply. 'Oh,' a voice cried, far down the room, 'that do 'urt . . . that do 'urt.' Geary felt peaceful. Among so many sufferers, he could rest for a while, allow full play to his own physical sufferings. But he must get away soon. The ill, the dispirited, the dying, were no real help to him.

The next morning, a policeman came to his bedside. A burly form, glasses taken out of a metal case, a clipboard.

'Now, perhaps you can help us with our enquiries. If we can have a description we'll soon have the man we want.'

Geary was ready. 'There were two of them. Both aged about thirty-five. I'd say they were professionals. Only one of them spoke; the other seemed to leave the talking to him by agreement. The one who spoke had a broad Lancashire accent.'

'H'm. Did he sound as if he was putting it on?'

'No, it sounded very genuine.'

'What were they wearing?'

'Raincoats. And caps pulled well down. One was fatter than the other, but I wouldn't have said either of them was noticeable in physique. Average height, average build.'

'Colour of hair?'

'They never took their caps off. They might have been bald for all I could tell.'

'And what happened?'

'They came and sat at my table, waited till the place was empty except for one old girl asleep, and then asked me for my wallet. The one with the Lancashire accent said, quite quietly, *Hand it over and nobody'll hurt you.* I tried to play for time, pretending to fumble for my wallet, and kept one eye on the door. But when I jumped up to make a run for it, they were ready for me. They both hit me at once.'

'With anything? Or just with their fists?'

'Only one blow. After that I was down and the rest was kicking.' A shadow of pain crossed Geary's face as the words reminded him of his aching ribs.

The policeman sat silent, reading over what he had written. At last he stood up, looked down at Geary, and said, 'Not much for us to go on, is there? And yet you'll expect us to find them.'

'I shan't blame you if you don't.'

'If you don't,' said the policeman, 'you'll be the first that ever didn't.'

He went away. Geary lay on his back, waiting to be released from the hospital, wondering if the policeman had known that he was lying. Then he shrugged, mentally. Lying or not, he must see to it that the Irishmen were not traced. If the police caught and prosecuted them, the trial would be attended by reporters. And Geary wanted no publicity. He wanted to be left in peace at the station.

Later that day, he took a taxi back to the hotel. An ambulance was ordered, but Geary got away before it arrived and drove up to the station hotel in a normal way. Only the stiffness with which he carried himself would have told a practised observer that his ribs were encased in plaster. He had arranged to attend the hospital as an out-patient for the necessary length of time. Before going up to his room, he walked stiffly across to the bookstall and bought another copy of the book he had been reading. He assumed that his other copy, splashed with blood and brushed to the floor of the refreshment room, had by now been thrown away.

'Geary's not in our gang,' said Julian Robinson.

'Yes, he is, then,' said a tall, freckled boy. 'He always has been.'

'Well, he's out now,' said Julian sullenly. He had had a disappointing morning, and felt the need to inflict suffering. 'He's too wet to be in our gang.'

'What have I done that's wet?' David Geary asked with a confidence he did not feel. Standing by the board fence near the school gate, he felt the unfriendliness of the street outside and the coldness of Robinson's eyes. The gang, five in number, looked from one to the other irresolutely.

'You're afraid to fight,' said Julian Robinson. 'Our gang's only for people who aren't afraid to fight, and you are.'

'You'd better fight him if you want to show he's afraid,' said the freckled boy.

'All right,' said Julian. He put his satchel down on the ground. 'Now or after afternoon school?' he asked David Geary.

'Why is it so important to fight?' David asked.

'You see,' said Julian, turning to the others, 'he's afraid.'

Suddenly scarlet with rage, David ran at him and dashed his fist into his face.

'I wasn't ready, you swine,' said Julian, backing. 'I'll kill you for that.'

'Come on then.'

The two fought savagely. They were not strong enough to break each other's bones, but they punched, elbowed, kicked and tore each other with a real lust to hurt. Then, exactly like two dogs, they seemed to lose interest in what they were doing. Verbal warfare succeeded.

'You can't fight fair.'

'I can fight better than you, anyway,' said David.

'It's even Stephen,' said the freckled boy, who was in a pacific mood.

'Well, he's not coming to gang meetings,' said Julian. He was only just not sobbing, with vexation and pain. 'He's wet. His whole family's wet. And his father's mad. He thinks we don't know, but we do. Everybody knows his father's mad, he's off his chump, he's bonkers.'

'What are you talking about?' David demanded. His heart was suddenly thumping in panic. This was an attack he could not deal with.

'I heard some grown-ups talking about it to my mother and father. They were talking about your father and saying he was mad. Then I heard my father ringing up a loony doctor and telling him your father was bonkers. He lives on the station and won't come off it. They're going to lock him up.'

'What station?'

'Paddington Station,' said Julian. 'Don't pretend you don't know. He spends all day there because he's mad, he's an idiot like you.'

David, grinning with hate, ran at Julian and seized him by the hair. 'Take it back!' he yelled, dragging his head from side to side. 'Take it back! Take it back!'

'Let go, you swine. I wasn't ready. Let go!'

'Take it back!' David screamed. 'Take it back!'

'I say, steady on,' said the freckled boy.

'Say, "Your father's sane". Go on, say it or I'll kill you.'

'I'll get you for this.'

'Say it.'

'Your father's sane.'

'Again.'

'Your father's sane.'

David released him. Julian stood back, rubbing his head, then suddenly sprang and tried to kick David in the crotch. But the tall boy with the freckles pushed him aside.

'That's enough!' he said sharply. 'Stop fighting now! That's enough!'

He was genuinely sickened at so much hatred and violence. Besides, he felt vaguely sorry for Geary. He did not doubt for an instant that Geary's father was mad. After all, everyone's father was mad in one way or another. His own father used to foam with rage, yes, actually foam, at things he read in the *Daily Telegraph*.

Elizabeth Geary had a serious problem. She could not decide whether or not to shorten the skirt of her cocktail suit. The suit was of cream-coloured velvet and became her remarkably well. It took years off her age, and after all there were not so many to take off. But that, in a way, was just the trouble. In her cocktail suit, and properly made up, she looked so young that it seemed odd to wear a skirt that covered her knees. Every woman under thirty-five had shortened her skirts to be in the fashion; to cover one's knees, however rock-like, was nowadays almost the mark of a grandmother. If the cream velvet suit brought her age down a few years, ought she not to take up the skirt a few inches? Or would that, by making her look slightly absurd, underline the fact that she was over forty and thus put the stolen years back on again?

She stood in front of the long mirror in her bedroom, alternately hoisting the skirt up and letting it down again, frowning critically and envying her daughter, whose long colt's legs were, this season, regularly displayed almost to fork-level. Normally, she was too well-balanced a woman to agonize about her appearance. She chose her clothes carefully, made the best of herself and let it go at that. But tomorrow evening she was to be confronted by a definite challenge. 'Drinks' were to be served by some socially-minded neighbour between six and eight; and the object was 'to meet' Adrian Swarthmore.

Back in the 1940s, before she married Arthur Geary and settled down to well-managed domesticity, Elizabeth had worked on a newspaper; not as a reporter, but as personal secretary to the editor. On this paper, which was a widely respected 'quality' edited with fine balance between London and a big provincial city, a number of young, eager, gifted people had worked in those post-war days. Stirring times, Elizabeth Geary now reflected. Big questions were in the air, England's voice was heeded; the country was still climbing shakily on to its feet after the terrific physical mauling of the war, but it still had moral authority; the lion's roar had not yet been drowned out by the louder roar of juke-boxes. All of them, back in those needle-sharp days, had felt a sense of purpose, but none more keenly than Adrian Swarthmore. Already, it had been clear, Adrian was impatient with the self-imposed restraints of a quality journalism that aimed itself at the few. 'You've got to get your message *over*,' he had been fond of saying, doubling one fist and driving it into the palm of the other hand. 'And that means— over to the man in the bus queue.'

Elizabeth had admired Adrian Swarthmore. His intense, serious face, with those strikingly high cheek-bones and full, mobile lips, came back to her now as she looked at her own face in the mirror. Adrian had lived for journalism. As a cow crops grass and single-mindedly converts it into milk, so he had cropped people, opinions, events, and single-mindedly converted them into publicity. He had not stayed with that paper for long; he had left before she did. Perhaps the gap left by Adrian's departure, the sense of flatness that descended when his thrusting presence was no longer felt, had made her more receptive to the quiet, still character of Arthur Geary, whom she had met at about the same time. Not that she had known Adrian well. He had taken her out for a drink a couple of times, when the paper had gone to bed and there was nothing to do in the office. Had she, in some deep recess of her being, hoped . . . Put it another way: if Adrian Swarthmore had made her a proposition, if he had gone for her as he so obviously went for that red-headed Glasgow girl in the lay-out department, or that American girl with whom, eventually, he disappeared in the direction of London . . . not that Elizabeth had ever been a girl to indulge in loose affairs. But with Adrian, it might have turned into something better than a loose affair. She surprised herself, suddenly, with the frank, immodest thought: it would have been worth trying anyway.

Blushing slightly at catching herself so unawares, Elizabeth Geary turned away from the mirror. She would leave her skirt where it was, and rely on true, essential femininity. Adrian

Swarthmore would be certain to remember her. His career had so obviously taught him the value of a good memory; he had associated with hundreds of people and he remembered every one of them. His rise had been spectacular. All these years, while she had been vegetating quietly by the side of the man who had now taken himself off and left her in this slough, Adrian Swarthmore had been climbing nimbly from stair to stair. He had become a popular columnist; had a brief adventure into Parliament; gained control of a number of local newspapers; built up an impressive medium-sized empire. But his true love was not business, was not even money. It was publicity. To this deity, his faithfulness was absolute. When television took command, he had immediately gone down on his knees to it, cultivating every television producer, however minor, being friendly and flattering to every television critic, accepting without demur any opportunity to appear on the screen, in the humblest and most trivial role. He would without hesitation interview visiting politicians, take part in quiz games, advertise dog biscuits or confront surly teen-agers.

This, had Elizabeth Geary known it, was the central tragedy of Adrian Swarthmore's life. For all his efforts, his career as a television personality had never quite got airborne. However much he smiled and acquiesced, exuding geniality, however much, deciding on a change of tactics, he blustered and sneered, others smiled more winningly, sneered more incisively. He was well known, of course; but, somehow, the key assignments did not go to him. He was a second-liner and people were beginning to notice the fact. What he needed was a big spotlight all to himself; say, the control of an important news series that would run for a whole winter. Give people time to get really accustomed to his face and voice. Then they would demand him constantly, as a matter of habit.

'Mother,' said Angela Geary, appearing suddenly in the doorway, 'why don't you shorten that skirt?'

'Because I'm not your age, darling,' said Mrs. Geary acidly.

'I don't see that that matters,' said Angela. 'Mrs. Corcoran goes about in skirts shorter than *mine*, and she's a *million*.'

While Elizabeth Geary was anxiously watching her knees in the mirror, and Arthur Geary was sitting calmly under the station clock, Adrian Swarthmore was fidgeting in the waiting-room of Consolidated Television Limited. The room contained several chairs made of plastic basket-work, and a low table covered with magazines, but Adrian Swarthmore was neither sitting in a chair nor reading a magazine. He was too tense to do anything but stand in the centre of the room. Had anyone else been waiting there, he might have felt obliged to simulate calm and unconcern, but, being alone, he fidgeted freely, making short dashes across the carpet, taking his glasses off and putting them back on again, flicking his fingers, and breathing in deeply through his nose in an effort to steady his nerves. He was waiting to see Sir Ben Warble.

Sir Ben Warble was the top, the very pinnacle, of Consolidated Television. He had already been very rich when commercial television was first introduced; in fact, some of the money that went to organizing the powerful Parliamentary lobby that forced it into existence was his money; and now he was very much richer still. People, or at any rate the sort of people who cultivated Sir Ben, lowered their voices in pure reverence when they spoke of his money.

Adrian Swarthmore had tried persistently to gain Sir Ben Warble's ear and had several times succeeded. Sir Ben had listened patiently to Swarthmore's plan for launching a new series of programmes that would spotlight people in the news. But that was all he had done. He had listened and made no answer, beyond indicating that Swarthmore had his permission to bring up the subject again at a more suitable time. This time must be the suitable time. It had to go through *now*.

'I can't wait any longer, Ben,' Adrian Swarthmore rehearsed in an undertone. 'I'm at the peak of my powers *now*. It's a waste to keep me on the shelf.' And, for practice, he smiled a sudden, dazzling smile.

Interviewing people was an important part of his job. He had trained himself in a technique of interviewing that had proved remarkably successful, both on camera and off camera—sometimes very off camera indeed. This technique was very simple. All you did was to concentrate entirely on the person you were

interviewing, banishing all other thoughts and attending with
all your might to the lightest word, the most fleeting change of
expression, shown by the victim. This conveyed to the victim
that nothing in the world mattered except what he, or she, might
be disposed to think, feel, say or do. The effect was like that of a
burning-glass. It was an unfailing method of putting on the heat.

Would it work with Sir Ben? It must work.

'I feel this is the moment, Ben,' Adrian Swarthmore went on,
in the same undertone. 'My instinct tells me I'm plugged in to the
mind of the public *now*, this minute. I know what interests them
and what'll keep them switched on. We'll get the best viewing figures in history. Well, I ask you, Ben. Have I ever been wrong? An
old news-hawk like me?' No, cut that. Leave the ending as it was
before, he decided.

'Will you come up now, Mr. Swarthmore?' asked a trim young
secretary, who had entered noiselessly from behind him and
must have overheard some, at least, of this last piece of persua-
sion. Following her as she glided across the hall to the lift, Adrian
Swarthmore shrugged. What did it matter if a chit of a girl had
heard him talking to himself? He had been practising for Ben, and
it had worked; he felt keyed up and ready to attack the citadel.

Sir Ben sat, watchful and heavy-lidded, in his office. His desk,
of light Swedish wood, was absolutely empty except for a big glass
ash-tray. Not even a blotter, not even a paper-weight. The impression was successfully conveyed that Sir Ben was too important to
do anything but sit at his desk and smoke cigars and knock the ash
into the big glass ash-tray. He had no need to write things down or
even to telephone anybody. All he did was think and smoke cigars.
The room was permanently scented with Havana smoke, and as
Swarthmore entered Sir Ben blew out a small cloud by way of
greeting.

'You know what I want, Ben,' said Swarthmore, after short salu-
tations had been exchanged and Sir Ben had waved him to a chair.
'That spotlight series. I'm all ready to go and I want to know when
we can firm it up.'

'You want to know that, do you?' Sir Ben returned. He sat
perfectly still, looking at Swarthmore's face.

'Look, Ben,' said Swarthmore. He passed the tip of his tongue over his lips. 'You've known me for a long time and you know I've always done what I've said I could do.' He swung into the main body of his rehearsed speech. It took ten minutes, during which Sir Ben never moved and never took his eyes off Swarthmore's face. 'I can't wait any longer, Ben,' Swarthmore finished. 'I'm at the peak of my powers *now*. It's a waste to keep me on the shelf.' He smiled, suddenly, dazzlingly.

There was a silence, then Sir Ben tapped a three-inch length of ash into the glass vessel, where it lay like the corpse of a small animal. 'All right, Adrian,' he said in his harsh, deliberate voice. 'Here's what we'll do. We won't plan a series ahead. We'll give you a guest spot in the existing newsreel programme. A spot you can take up at any time. If you get a scoop, we'll make room for it right away, that same evening.'

'But I can get a scoop every week, Ben. You know that. It's fifty years since newsmen sat about and waited for scoops. They go out and make them happen. If I had a weekly spot, I'd turn in a weekly scoop. Surely you've—'

'I don't mean that kind of scoop,' said Sir Ben, his voice riding effortlessly over Swarthmore's. He leaned forward and gave a pleasant smile. 'I mean a real scoop. The first time you get one, we'll open up the newsreel programme that same evening and slot you into it. You can have two cameramen on fifteen minutes' notice at any time, ready to go out. Then you can direct the whole thing— filming, editing, and doing interviews with the people concerned.'

'Can the inset have a title? Can we put a frame round it so that the viewer doesn't think it's just run-of-the-mill newsreel stuff? A title like, say, *The Swarthmore Eye?*'

'If it's a real scoop,' said Sir Ben, 'it'll stand out and you'll get your credits. If it isn't one—'

'It will be, Ben,' said Adrian Swarthmore quickly.

The interview was concluded.

The telephone beside Geary's bed gave a long, imperious ring. Geary, his face dark with stubble, stirred and shivered. Still asleep, he moved the bedclothes up round his ears and buried his head more deeply in the pillow. But the telephone rang again.

Slowly, Geary's arm crept out from the bedclothes and lifted the receiver. His eyes opened and became wary.

'Hello.'

'Mr. Geary, I have a call for you. You're through, go ahead, please.'

'Mr. Geary?' said a man's voice.

'Yes.'

'I hope you'll forgive my disturbing you so early,' said the voice. It sounded both courteous and assured.

'What time is it?' asked Geary.

'Eight o'clock. Five past, to be precise.'

'Oh,' said Geary. He sat up. 'I'm still in bed, I'm afraid.'

A chuckle. 'So would I be, if I hadn't got to catch a train this morning. But let me introduce myself. My name is Maurice Blakeney.'

'Blakeney?' said Geary. He held the telephone more tightly.

'Yes, I don't think we've ever met, but we've been neighbours, more or less, for some years. I'm at the Charles Grayson Hospital.'

'Yes,' said Geary. 'The Grayson.' He looked about the room as if measuring the chances of escape. Then he stiffened, composed his face into a calm expression, and said, 'What can I do for you, Dr. Blakeney?'

'Well,' said Blakeney. He hesitated for a moment. 'It sounds like an unwarrantable intrusion, but I was wondering if you could spare a few minutes to talk to me this morning,'

'Certainly,' said Geary. 'But may I ask what you want to talk about?'

'Well,' said Blakeney again. 'Some friends of yours have asked me to put one or two questions to you. I promise not to take more than a few minutes of your time. You see, I'm coming to town today, on business, and I shall be on the train that gets in at eleven-fifteen. If you'd allow me to come to the hotel and look you up, I'll be as brief as possible.'

'I may not be in the hotel,' said Geary. 'I've got a lot of things to do this morning.' He thought for a moment. 'Well, yes, perhaps

I could . . . rearrange things a bit. All right, come along at eleven-fifteen when your train gets in. I'll be in the hotel lobby.'

'Thank you. We don't know each other by sight, so I'll go and stand by the reception desk when I get there. I'll be wearing a grey mackintosh and carrying a copy of *The Times*. Is that all right?'

'Perfectly,' said Geary. 'A lot of people who get off that train are wearing grey mackintoshes and carrying *The Times*. But they won't all be standing at the reception desk. I'll find you all right.'

Blakeney thanked him and rang off. Geary lay back on his pillow, thinking. The cold, greasy light of a November day filtered into the room.

After a while, Geary rang for room service and took breakfast in bed. Then, after a bath and a long, scrupulous shave, he dressed carefully, selecting his clothes with great deliberation. At intervals he muttered to himself. 'You are calm,' he said softly. 'You are balanced. You are in complete control.'

At eleven-fifteen he went downstairs to the hotel lobby. There, he sat in an armchair, reading a newspaper. He was the picture of calm, organized composure. Occasionally he glanced up from his newspaper; after six or seven minutes, one of these glances revealed Dr. Blakeney, wearing his grey raincoat and carrying a copy of *The Times*, standing beside the reception desk.

Before rising, Geary studied the man for a few seconds. This was the opponent who must be vanquished utterly, driven from the field at the first encounter.

Dr. Maurice Blakeney was a tall, fleshy man with an air of confidence and good humour. His face was round and pink, and he wore rimless glasses. At first glance, he was sometimes taken for a Central European; he had in fact studied in Vienna and Berlin. But the impression of foreignness did not last beyond a few moments. The ease and assurance with which he spoke and moved his limbs, the complete confidence of ascendancy that looked out from behind his lenses, could only have been found in an Englishman from the upper middle classes who was over fifty years of age and had long been accustomed to authority.

'You are calm,' Geary said to himself, 'you are balanced,' and he went over and said, 'Dr. Blakeney?'

Blakeney turned, unsurprised. 'Ah, Mr. Geary. It's good of you to spare me a few minutes.'

'Shall we have some coffee?' said Geary levelly. When Blakeney assented, he rang the bell, settled himself into an armchair, and invited Blakeney to sit beside him.

'Now,' he said comfortably, 'what would you like to ask me?'

'I'd better come straight to the point,' said Blakeney. He gave a small, deprecating smile. 'Some friends of yours are worried about you. They can't quite reassure themselves that everything's quite all right with you. And they've asked me to talk to you and give my opinion as a doctor.'

'In other words,' Geary smiled, relaxed, 'they want to know whether I'm sane or not.'

Blakeney shrugged pleasantly. 'Which of us is truly sane, in this mad muddle we've built for ourselves? But some people can benefit by certain kinds of help.'

'And you're going to decide what kind of help I need?'

Blakeney glanced at Geary with a grave, appraising expression. 'You may not need any,' he said. 'But these friends of yours are people I respect and I thought their concern for you was something I ought to take seriously.'

'It does them credit,' Geary said simply.

The waiter arrived and was despatched for coffee. When he had gone, Blakeney settled himself more deeply into his chair and said, 'You spend a lot of time in this hotel, don't you?'

'I'm staying here at present.'

'I suppose it's as convenient a place as any,' said Blakeney carefully. 'I've heard, of course, that you're living apart from your wife.'

'My marriage is washed up,' said Geary. 'I decided to move to town while I thought what to do next. I imagine it's what most people would do under my circumstances.'

'You're sure the break-up is permanent? It isn't something that could be sorted out?'

Geary shook his head. 'I accept the responsibility. It was I, not

my wife, who found the marriage increasingly intolerable. I held
on as long as I could and when I decided it was the end, I knew it
really was the end.'

Blakeney paused, considering. 'You think you'll marry again?'

'There's no one in my life at the moment. What the future
might bring I can't say.'

The coffee arrived, and conversation halted while it was poured
out, sugared, stirred. Then Blakeney said, 'If you don't mind my
asking you one or two questions . . .'

'Of course not. Go ahead.'

'I understand you've given up your job at the Institute.'

'Yes.'

'Does that mean you're without income at the moment?'

Geary smiled. 'A careful, conventional type like me doesn't get
to the age of forty-five without having a bit salted away. I shan't
starve, and neither will my family, while I look about for a bit.'

'You'll take another post somewhere?'

'Naturally,' said Geary. He drank from his cup and set it carefully down.

Blakeney decided to move in to the attack.

'You see,' he said, 'your actions obviously seem very rational
from your own point of view, but your friends are worried because
they see them rather differently. In particular, your habit of spending all your time on the station.'

Geary looked up, wide-eyed. 'On the station?'

'Yes, they say you never leave the station except to come into
the hotel.'

Geary laughed without strain. 'Who are these friends?'

'I was wondering when you'd ask me that.'

'Well, I thought you'd tell me in your own good time if you
were going to. And I wasn't very curious. But really—if there are
people going about under the impression that I'm a madman, I
ought to know who they are.'

'Is it true,' said Blakeney quietly, 'that you never move off the
station?'

'It's utter fantasy,' said Geary. 'I'm staying here because it's a
comfortable, well-run hotel and because I still have a number of

things to clear up at the Institute. It's handy for the trains and central enough for most of the things I want to do in town. Of course I'm seen on the platform now and then. If I go to the refreshment room for a glass of beer, that's because the stuff costs twice as much in the cocktail bar here. Or I might go to the newsstand for a paper, or the barber's for a hair-cut. The streets round here aren't exactly pleasant enough to go for a stroll in. My world, at present, is this hotel and its immediate neighbourhood. And that means the station. But I must say it's disconcerting to find oneself described as a lunatic who's got some kind of obsession with the station and can't leave it.'

'So you *can* leave it?'

'As easily as you can,' said Geary.

'Well,' said Blakeney, 'that wraps it up, I suppose. You're staying at this hotel while you look for another job, you move about quite freely, it's a sheer illusion that you're spending your life on the station. In fact your main motive for being here is because you expect to be catching trains down to the Institute.'

'Yes,' said Geary.

'Have you actually been down there since you came to town?'

'Not yet.'

Maurice Blakeney stood up. 'Well, I needn't take any more of your time,' he said. 'I'll tell Philip Robinson that everything's all right.'

'Philip Robinson,' said Geary, grinning. 'I thought as much. He's a nice chap. But over-anxious, always has been. Give him my best regards. I appreciate his worrying about me, but do tell him to relax.'

'I will,' said Blakeney. He smiled, buttoned his mackintosh, and was gone.

For some minutes Geary sat quite still in his chair. Then, slowly, he rose and went towards the lift. It was engaged, and he pressed the button and waited. The lift came down, people got out and walked away. Geary stood facing the empty lift, its doors wide open. But he made no attempt to enter it and go up to his room. He stood looking at it, saying quietly to himself, 'You are calm. You are balanced. You are under complete control.'

Geary knew that he ought to go up to his room and wait there for a while, to give Maurice Blakeney time to get clear of the station. The lift was ready to take him up. But he hesitated, his lips moving, and finally someone on another floor summoned the lift, its doors closed and it moved upwards out of sight.

Geary, his face suddenly damp with sweat, turned and hurried out on to the platform. He moved to where the crowd was thickest and stood, close to the ticket-barrier, with people all round him. A party of excited schoolboys surged past, jostling him. A porter bumped his legs with a suitcase. Gradually, his heart slowed down and he stood there, calmly, looking about. There was no sign of Maurice Blakeney.

The immediate danger was over. But Geary could still not quite relax. He realized that Maurice Blakeney would probably be making another appearance on the station later that day, when he came to catch his train home. There was no knowing when this would be. If he was simply spending a working day in London and going home for dinner, he would be back on the station at about six. If, on the other hand, he stayed in town for a dinner-party or a theatre, he would not turn up again until nearly midnight, by which time Geary would be safely in bed.

The day was spoilt. In his level, matter-of-fact way, Geary faced the fact and accepted it. He would have to make himself inconspicuous and keep a sharp look-out for Blakeney. Better to have his peace interrupted for one day than risk having it destroyed for ever. Walking slowly, calculating, he moved over to the refreshment room. As he walked he became aware, suddenly, that his cracked ribs were aching in their uncomfortable sheath of plaster. Curses on that brute of an Irishman: for the first time, Geary thought of the man with a stab of real hate. Previously, he had seemed like something impersonal: a natural calamity, a piece of bad luck: like a windstorm that brought a tree crashing down on the road as he was walking by. Now, for an instant, the Irishman and Maurice Blakeney became entwined in Geary's mind: both hunters, trying to drive him from the forest glade where he had made his legitimate home, and both equally pitiless.

On his way to the refreshment room, Geary stopped and

bought a newspaper. Then he collected a cup of coffee and went to a corner seat, which he turned sideways so as to get his back to the wall. Now he felt secure. No one could come suddenly round from behind him, and he was in a position to see everyone who came in at the door. At the first sign of danger, he could retire behind his newspaper. Without having to face the unnerving solitude of his hotel room, he was safe from attack by Maurice Blakeney or anyone else.

One problem remained. His fastness was only a temporary one. The refreshment room was busy, and to sit too long over one cup of coffee earned him unfriendly looks from the staff. Already, he fancied that the two West Indians who moved ceaselessly about with trolleys, clearing away crockery and wiping the tables, were beginning to look over at him and mutter remarks to one another. Certainly they never passed each other without exchanging a word or two, and he was sure that one of them, at least, kept glancing in his direction.

Sternly immobile, Geary hoisted his newspaper. In its shelter, he looked at his watch. Twenty minutes. Surely a cup of coffee entitled him to at least half an hour. Lowering the newspaper with an air of unconcern, he sat on, his empty cup beside him, for ten more minutes. Then he stood up. Neither West Indian had so far made any move to clear his table. The coffee-cup stood at his elbow like some defiant symbol of an Englishman's liberty.

A Frenchman, of course, would have had no problem. Continental customs permitted a man to sit all morning in a café over a cup of something. But would that be the same in a big Parisian railway station? For a moment, Geary had a wild vision of catching a boat-train and going to the Gare du Nord for a month. The vision faded as he remembered all the complications: the journey across London to get to the boat-train, the visits to the bank for foreign currency, the packing, the departure from his comfortable eyrie in the hotel, the anxiety about rebooking. He also found himself recoiling from the journey itself. It was not trains he liked, it was stations. And not just any station: only this one, or one very like it. The Gare du Nord would do, but only if he could transport himself there by magic. And only for a month, at the outside.

Geary stood up. Why was he permitting himself these disqui-
eting thoughts? 'You are in complete control,' he said quietly to
himself, folding up his paper into a neat parallelogram. He went
over to the counter for a refill; his stomach revolted at the thought
of more coffee, so he bought himself a bowl of hot soup and a
piece of white bread. Turning, he saw a fat, ill-dressed woman in
the very act of lowering herself into his corner seat.

Fighting down panic, holding his bread and soup in unnaturally
steady hands, Geary looked round for a seat. There were several unoccupied, but none that would do. All the secure places,
in good cover, were occupied. 'You are calm,' he said to himself.
Without hesitation, he put down his bread and soup on the nearest
table. Anyone who happened to be watching him would get the
impression that he was setting them down momentarily while he
went over to move a suitcase or overcoat to a safer place. Then,
without pausing or looking back, he walked out on to the platform.

Where was safety? He thought of the hotel, then shuddered
briefly. Not till night. It was all right at night, when he could lie
down and sleep, knowing that all round him eight million others
were lying down too. But if he stayed on the platform he was
wide open to Blakeney's appraising, probing eyes. The platform
. . . which platform? Across on the other side of the station was a
strange, dark hinterland, a platform inhabited only by the railway
staff, with a series of openings that seemed to lead to dark caverns.
He would be safe there, and surely any employee who saw him
would imagine that he was some inspector or other legitimate
person. Stepping with brisk dignity, he crossed the station foyer,
went past the taxicab rank, and walked down the long platform
under the notices that said 'STAFF ONLY'.

For an hour, Geary moved about from one archway to another.
Railwaymen moved crates about, hurried past him with sheaves of
papers held together by bulldog clips, drove processions of small
wagons up and down. The peace was delicious. Geary stood, arms
folded and legs apart, savouring his immunity. Then he felt a sharp
tap on the shoulder and turned to see a pair of suspicious eyes
under a peaked cap.

'May I ask,' the voice was narrow and cockney, but with the

habit of some minor authority, 'whether you're a member of British Railways staff?'

'No,' said Geary.

'What are you then . . . may I ask?'

'A passenger,' said Geary.

'Oh, a passenger, eh? May I see your ticket?'

'I've given it up.'

'You've given up your ticket, and you haven't got a return half, so you're not going back anywhere, and you've spent an hour standing about on the platform that isn't open to the public. Can you read?'

'Yes,' said Geary.

The man looked at him with fierce self-satisfaction. 'Look, friend, I just want you to know that you're not fooling anybody.'

'I'm not trying to fool anybody.' Inwardly Geary said, 'You are calm. You are in complete control.'

'We've seen your bloody sort before.'

'My sort?'

'Don't play the innocent with me. Charley!' The man raised his voice imperiously. A red-haired porter, his short jacket skimpy over a burly back and shoulders, came out from the cavern behind them.

'We were right, Charley. He's one of 'em.'

'Hold him while we get the union official,' said Charley promptly.

Geary felt panic rising uncontrollably in his chest. The plaster carapace seemed to be roasting his ribs. 'I don't know what you mean,' he said in a quick, high voice.

The first man reached out and caught Geary's elbow in a hard grasp. 'All right, Charley boy, get on the phone. Tell him we've got one of these time and motion bastards breaking the union agreement.'

'I'm *not*,' cried Geary. 'If you get the union down here you'll find you've just made a fool of yourself. I've nothing to do with all that.'

'I'll risk it. Go on, Charley.'

'I seen him before,' said Charley, who was now looking attentively at Geary. 'I seen him on the platforms, nosing about.'

'Of course you've seen me on the platforms,' said Geary desperately. 'I'm a regular commuter.'

'In that case,' said the first man, calmly, 'show us your season ticket.'

Geary, his elbow released, took out his wallet. Smoothly, holding his fingers steady, he selected two crisp one-pound notes. He held one out to Charley, who wordlessly took it. The first challenger, however, kept his arms by his sides.

'You can't bribe your way out of this.'

'It's not bribery,' said Geary. 'It's just my way of making an apology. I can see I've annoyed you men and aroused your suspicions. You took me for some kind of nark. Well, the fact is I'm just a harmless nut.' He grinned, unjoined.

'A nut?' said Charley.

'I'm a railway fanatic,' said Geary, 'and my special interest is in station administration. I'm writing a book on how the big stations organize themselves. You say you've seen me,' he turned to Charley, 'hanging about the platforms. Well, I'm to be seen hanging about the platforms on every main-line station in the country. I'm nothing to do with time and motion or anything like that.' He held out the pound note. 'Go on, take my apology. It's well-meant.'

The man accepted the note, stood looking at it for a moment, then folded it and put it in his pocket. 'We have to be careful,' he said, looking steadily at Geary.

'Of course you do.'

'I'm not sure I believe you, even now.'

'You will,' Geary smiled, 'when my book comes out.'

'What's your name?'

'Roger Lloyd,' said Geary.

Charley turned his broad back dismissively and walked back into the shadows. The other man stood, reluctant to let the matter drop, but tamed by the pound note in his pocket.

'Better not hang about here, anyway.'

'I'll go now,' said Geary cheerfully. 'I was just getting . . . an impression. I don't need to stay any longer.'

Under the man's hard stare, he turned and walked casually back to the station foyer. Then, in case the eyes were still on him, he kept going and went down to the underground railway. Halting by the row of ticket-machines, he pretended to be scrutinizing them, looking for the name of a particular station. A large, matronly coloured woman was collecting tickets; she glanced over at him protectively, and seemed about to ask if he needed help. Nervously, he sidled away, and presently chose a moment when the woman was busy to walk rapidly back the way he had come.

He went up the steps to the station foyer. It was barely lunch-time. How was he going to get through the rest of the day? Where could he hide from the ever-present threat of Blakeney? Was every-one watching him?

Well, there was always his room. He could stand the solitude for an hour or two. Take an interesting book up with him. Then terror came again. They might be watching the room. Better keep away from it till nightfall. What did that Eliot poem say? 'Put your boots outside the door, sleep, prepare for life.' That was it.

Resolutely, calming himself, Geary went to the more crowded of the refreshment rooms and stood in a long queue to get to the counter. There, he bought a meat pie and a bottle of beer, and moved over to a place near the window. He would eat standing up, so that he could move unobtrusively if he had to. Getting up from a chair was apt to attract attention.

Chewing, gulping the fizzy beer, he stared out at the station. The light from the outside world came filtering down as if through porcelain. People hurried past with closed faces, intent on the comings and goings that made up their lives. The stream thickened: a train had just arrived. New arrivals, carrying brief-cases or moving awkwardly with heavy bags, made for the underground. A few peeled off and came into the refreshment room. People, people, a lovely thick anonymous stream of humanity. Then one face stood out: small, irresolute. A little figure in a blue mackintosh, going in no direction, looking uneasily about, a small question-mark on the dark, shifting page of the station: and Geary recognized his son, David.

Was this a dream? If so, he must act within the dream as he would act in real life. Quickly setting down his glass, Geary went out through the door and overtook the slowly wandering boy.

'David,' he said in a calm, quiet voice.

David spun round. He was obviously unnerved at being recognized first. If he had any rehearsed greeting or opening speech, he forgot it now. His face flushed, then went pale, and he gulped.

'Dad, hello. I'm just . . . it's—'

Geary smiled warmly, covering everything with one overlaying blanket of welcome.

'Come in here and have something to eat. I expect you could do with something.'

'Yes. I haven't had lunch.'

Geary became all solicitude. 'Never mind the buffet, then. Come into the hotel and we'll fix you up with a proper lunch.' His voice uttered the bright, quick words without effort, almost without volition; his feet walked automatically towards the hotel entrance. A hungry boy, a kindly father, a hot meal; it was easy to fend off what lay beyond.

David was silent until they were settled at a table in the dining-room, then he asked, 'Are you staying here?'

'Yes,' said Geary.

'For long?'

'That depends. As long as it takes me to get things settled.'

David looked at him with deep, serious eyes. 'What kind of things?'

If Geary had wanted to be completely candid in his answer to this he would have said, 'The drums.' For some months past he had been troubled by a feeling that drums were being beaten inside his head and chest. These drums had both sound and vibration; sometimes they sounded as if they were being softly stroked, at other times gently and slowly beaten with muffled sticks, and at other times beaten very hard and very fast. Sometimes, in the last weeks of their marriage, he had lain on his back in the early morning, with Elizabeth sleeping beside him, and heard the drums beating so frenziedly that he could not understand why Elizabeth was not woken by them.

He might have told David that once, during this bad time, he had paid a visit to London, and found when he arrived at the station a little early for his train home, and waited quietly in the buffet, that the drums did not beat while he was there. He listened and listened, but he did not hear them. They only started up when he was sitting in the train and it began to pull out. After that the idea of staying on the station, away from the sound of the drums, had grown and grown in his mind.

He might have told David about the drums. But he did not. Instead, he shrugged and said, 'Oh, just—details. Where I'm going to be, what I'm going to do.'

'Dad,' said David suddenly, 'why don't you want to be with us?'

'D'you want to order, sir?' asked the waitress, who had soundlessly appeared at Geary's elbow.

Geary ordered a good meal for David and for himself half a bottle of wine. 'To celebrate,' he explained. 'It's an unexpected pleasure to see you.'

The waitress departed. David sat silent, looking at the tablecloth. He was obviously thrown by having no reply to the direct question he had screwed himself up to ask.

'Look, David,' said Geary gently. 'Before you ask me any questions, there's one I'd like to ask you.'

The boy waited, mute and guarded.

'What was your idea in coming here?'

'To find you.'

'Who told you you'd find me here?'

David picked up a fork, looked at it, and put it down. 'I wanted to talk to you.'

'So you came here,' said Geary. 'But why here? To the station? Something must have given you the idea that I was here.'

David looked mutinous. 'Well, I was right, wasn't I?'

The waitress arrived with David's soup and Geary's half-bottle of expensive wine, canted over in a basket. Gravely, Geary went through the motions of pouring a little of the wine into a glass, tasting it, and nodding to the waitress. She filled his glass and departed.

'Cheers,' said Geary to David. He drank a little and set his glass down. 'David, there's nothing to be upset about, old son. I know it's a change for you not to have me about the place, and it'll take a bit of getting used to at first, but we'll be in touch and you'll see me as often as you like. Just because I'm not living in the house doesn't mean I'm not still your father, you know.' He drank again, bracing himself. 'It's—better as it is. One day I'll try and tell you all about it. That's a promise.'

David finished his soup. He appeared not to hear his father. But suddenly, setting down his spoon in his empty plate, he looked full at Geary and said, 'Why are you living on the station? That's what I don't—'

'Who told you that?' asked Geary quickly. His ribs ached: the plaster seemed to be crushing the life out of him.

'If I tell you that, will you tell me why you're doing it?'

Geary hesitated for an instant, then said, 'Yes.'

'I heard it from a boy at school,' said David, leaning forward. The waitress put a dish of braised steak in front of him, but he ignored it. His eyes were trained on his father's face. 'He said you were,' he hesitated, 'spending all your time on the station.'

'Potatoes, sir?' said the waitress to David. She was in a hurry to get on to her other tables, and she was not free to do so until David had chosen some vegetables.

'Better take some,' said Geary. 'The cabbage looks good too.'

David helped himself mechanically. When they were alone, he tried again. 'This boy said you were—'

'Who was this boy, anyway? What's his name?'

'Julian Robinson.'

Geary thought. 'That must be Philip Robinson's son.'

'I don't know what his father's called. But he came up to me in the school yard and said to me *Your father's mad.*' Frightened, he looked down. The words were out at last.

Three times, Geary thought. Blakeney, then the railwayman, now this. How long could he hold on? Three attacks in one morning.

'Did you believe him?' he asked.

David, still looking down at the table, shook his head.

'Did he give any reason for saying I was mad?'

'He said you never left the station. He said you spent all your time walking about on it and you couldn't act normally any more.'

'Don't I seem to you,' Geary asked gently, 'to be acting normally?'

'I don't know,' said David. His face suddenly puckered and he pushed his plate aside. 'I can't eat,' he whimpered.

'Listen, David, don't worry. I don't know what fantastic story that boy had got hold of. I'm in my right mind, as you can surely see.'

'I don't mind for myself,' said David, his voice soft and strangled. 'It isn't that I mind them saying my father's mad. I was just worried for you, that's all.'

Geary finished the rest of his wine in a long, reckless draught. He forced himself into calm, smiled and said, 'Well now, eat your lunch and we'll go up to my room. I'll show you where I'm living and I'll explain what I'm doing. Will that make you feel better?'

'Yes,' said David. He blew his nose and added, 'I feel quite hungry.'

'Get a good lunch,' Geary smiled. 'The cooking's not bad here.'

When David had eaten they went up in the lift. Geary's room, with its carpet, curtains and bedspread in well-chosen matching colours, and its neat bathroom glinting through the half-open door, seemed the essence of workaday common sense.

'You see, David,' said Geary, sinking into the armchair, 'this hotel is very central, and well-run without being tremendously expensive. It suits me very well to stay here till I've got everything cleared up.' Without pausing to give David a chance to question him on this he added quickly, 'Does anyone know you're here, by the way?'

'Only you.'

'I meant anyone at home.'

David shook his head. 'I'm not going to ask Mother any more. If I decide it's right to do a thing I'll just do it.'

Geary looked stern. 'You're not old enough to take the law into your own hands, my lad.'

'I thought,' said David carefully, 'that if it was all right for you to leave home *for ever* because you didn't want to stay, it was all right for me to come away for *one day*.'

'Our cases are rather different.'

'I don't see why.'

Geary did not see why either, so he made no reply to this.

'Anyway,' he said, 'I'll put you on a train home before they get worried about you. There's a good one at four-fifteen.'

'How long's that from now?'

Geary looked at his watch. 'About an hour.'

'You want to get rid of me, don't you?' said David bitterly.

'I just don't want them to get worried at home,' said Geary. Then, catching sight of the boy's distressed face, he went on more softly, 'David, please don't worry. Whatever happens I'll take care of you and see that you don't go short of anything. And every time you want to ask or tell me anything, you can come and see me.'

'Will you be here?'

'Wherever I am,' said Geary, 'I'll see to it that you know my address.' He took out his wallet. 'This is for fares,' he said. 'Keep it on one side.' He handed David a five-pound note. 'Where did you get the money from this morning, by the way?'

'From my Christmas fund,' said David. 'It left me pretty cleaned out, and I only got a single ticket.'

'You only got a single ticket?' Geary repeated. 'Suppose you'd missed me. How were you proposing to get back?'

'I was just going to stay here till I *did* see you,' said David. He looked away. 'I miss you an awful lot.'

Something seemed to break inside Geary. It was as if, inside his chest, he had been carrying his feelings in carefully contrived glass containers. Now the containers shattered and his chest was flooded with blood, mush and broken glass. He opened his mouth to say something, but the possibilities jammed his brain. He wanted to say that he would leave the station and come home with David, then and there. He wanted to invite David to move into the hotel with him. He wanted to explain to David about the drums. He wanted to promise David that he would leave the station hotel within a week and find a place to live where David could come and stay in every school holiday. Beyond all these things he wanted to say something that would lift the cold weight from David's heart, and from his own. Nothing came and he allowed his mouth to close, drooping at the corners. Father and son looked at each other across the impersonal furniture.

'Will you ever come home?' David said in a whisper.

'David,' said Geary. His voice was dry; the name sounded in the room like the creak of a shed door. 'I promise you here and now that I'll make everything all right. I'll have things on a . . . better footing.' This sounded unconvincing. But it was too late, now, to tell David the truth. He began again. 'You'll see. I have to put my life into a new shape, but it'll be a shape that you'll be able to . . . to understand and share. I promise you, David.'

The boy's face brightened a little. But his eyes were still troubled; he still looked across at Geary as if begging for something tangible to take away with him.

Geary felt desperate. The blood and broken glass were churning about inside his chest. He loved David. He must reach the boy; he must, must reach him.

'Look at this,' he said suddenly. Pulling off his jacket, he began snatching at his shirt buttons. Shirt and vest came off: the white plaster gleamed in the despondent light.

David sprang up. 'What on earth—'

Geary slapped the plaster. 'I had a little accident. Fell over and cracked a couple of ribs. That's one reason why I can't move out of this neighbourhood for a week or two yet. I'm an out-patient at the hospital down the road.'

In horrified pity, David examined the plaster. 'Does it hurt?'

'It ached a bit at first. I didn't get much sleep for a night or two. It's all right now, though.'

'How did you do it?'

'I slipped at the top of a flight of steps. There must have been a banana skin there, or a piece of greasy paper or something. Anyway, by the time I got to the bottom I'd cracked two ribs, both on the same side.'

'Did somebody pick you up?'

'I got up myself,' said Geary. Suddenly feeling a little ashamed of his exhibition, he dressed quickly. 'So you see,' he said with a wry smile, 'there's one little bit of business that keeps me here, even if the others didn't.'

David walked springily over to the window. 'I feel a lot better,' he announced. 'Seeing you like this, and knowing about your accident, it . . . it . . .'

'It makes sense?' Geary supplied.

'Yes, it does.'

Relieved, they smiled at one another. The churning inside Geary's chest had stopped. He even felt that the glass compartments might knit together just as his ribs would.

'Well,' he said, glancing at his watch, 'we might as well get down to the station.'

'Already?'

'There's plenty to do,' said Geary. 'We must find out what platform your train goes from, then buy you a ticket. Then you can choose any book you like from the stall. By the time we've done all that and put a cup of tea inside you, the train'll be about ready to go.' He buttoned his jacket and moved towards the door. The empty air of the room was beginning to oppress him. 'Off we go,' he said.

David followed more slowly. 'Will you write to me?' he asked.

'Every week,' said Geary light-heartedly.

'Specially when your ribs get better?'

'I'll send you a telegram on the day the plaster comes off.'

They both laughed. On their laughter they moved easily, as if on rollers, down the corridor and into the lift. Without pausing, Geary led the way across the hotel foyer and on to the station.

There, as the pair of them sauntered amid the incessant tidal washing of the crowd, he breathed easily again. His problems, after all, were soluble. David would feel happier. The bond between them, temporarily snapped, was mended. Even the Irishman had had his part in the work of healing, by providing him with an objective reason for staying in the hotel. He glanced with approval at the fair-haired boy walking by his side. Then he saw Blakeney.

The doctor's lenses were gleaming as he stood under one of the electric lights which, at that season of the year, shone all day long. He must have arrived early for the train home, that same four-fifteen on which Geary planned to put David. Would they meet? Would Blakeney question the child, at his leisure, during a seventy-minute journey?

Geary stopped dead. The two must be kept apart. It would be easy enough to watch Blakeney, to see him safely installed on the train, before David—

Then the worst happened. Blakeney, who was about twenty-five yards away, turned and saw them.

'David,' said Geary quickly, 'we'd better just . . .' He looked round. The enquiry office was close at hand. 'We'll just ask in here, what platform your—'

'There's a notice here,' said David. 'That'll tell us.' He moved over and began to examine the printed list of train departures. Obviously it pleased him to be so grown-up and capable.

'I don't trust those lists,' said Geary, his throat very dry. 'They're . . . they're liable to alteration at short notice.' He pretended not to see that Blakeney was majestically bearing down on them. 'I think the enquiry office would be . . .' Agonized, he shifted from one foot to the other.

'Here it is,' said David, proud of himself. 'Platform One. It goes from here, Dad. Right where we're standing. I expect it'll be in soon.' He craned to see up the line.

'That's good,' said Geary. 'Well, let's go and get your ticket. Mustn't dawdle,' he added sharply. Blakeney was almost on him when he took David's arm and walked quickly along the platform, not away from Blakeney but towards him, right under his nose.

'What's the hurry, Dad?' David protested.

'We meet again,' said Blakeney genially.

'Ah hah,' Geary assented, hurrying past.

They left the platform and reached the safety of the booking hall.

'We've got ages yet, Dad.'

Geary glanced over his shoulder. 'David, did you see that man? The one who spoke to us?'

'With glasses? Just now?'

'That's the one,' said Geary. His breath was coming quickly. He took out a handkerchief and wiped sweat from his face. 'I want you to remember what I say, David. Don't talk to that man.'

'I don't even know him.'

'He may be on your train,' said Geary in a low voice. 'If he asks you any questions, don't answer. Just get up from your seat and go to another part of the train. You can go to the restaurant car if you like—I'll give you the money so you won't have to break into your five-pound note. But if he comes and sits down by you, move to another table or go back to your compartment. *Don't speak to him.*'

David nodded, round-eyed. He felt awed by the presence of large-scale, adult passions. He had wandered into the arena of these giants; it made him feel important and at the same time terribly vulnerable.

'I'll keep away from him, Dad.' He felt that he could not question his father on this huge, urgent matter.

Geary bought David's ticket. There were still twenty minutes to kill. The train clanked idly in to the platform, but he did not dare let David join it. That would be serving him up to Blakeney on a plate. Unless—he brightened as an idea occurred to him.

'Come on, David. I'll sit in the train with you till it goes. We'll be able to talk comfortably without running any risk of missing it.'

David hesitated. 'What if the man gets on?'

'He won't come near you while I'm with you.'

Geary was wrong. Soon after he and David had settled themselves in the train, Dr. Blakeney came along the platform. David was sitting by the window, and when Blakeney drew level he noticed the boy. An interested expression appeared on his face and he stopped.

'He's seen me, Dad.' David was frightened.

'It doesn't matter,' said Geary. He realized that he must have given David the impression that Blakeney was a child-murderer or perhaps a vampire.

'But he's looking at me.'

Blakeney, with an encouraging smile, had moved nearer to the window. Then he caught sight of Geary. His smile did not fade, but it became more hooded and discreet.

'Just let him come in here, that's all,' said Geary between his teeth.

Blakeney disappeared. Doubtless he was walking along to the door at the end of the coach. Geary sat motionless in his seat, every muscle tense. He felt the damp skin of his chest pushing hopelessly against the plaster.

'What will you do if he does come in?' David asked.

The question steadied Geary's mind. 'He isn't dangerous, David,' he said quietly. 'I mean, he won't do you any harm. All he'll do is to put questions to you, if he gets half a chance. Questions about me.'

'But I don't know anything about you.'

'There are things he wants to know that you can tell him. And I don't want him told anything.'

'Is he an enemy of yours, Dad?'

Blakeney appeared, looking down at them, in the doorway of the compartment.

'Yes,' said Geary softly.

'Ah, Mr. Geary,' said Blakeney in a pleased tone. He slid the door further open. 'I didn't realize you were travelling down today.' He moved in, and made as if to put his brief-case on the rack. 'D'you mind if I join you?'

'I'd rather you didn't, if you don't mind,' said Geary abruptly.

'Oh?' Blakeney was bland, unshakeable. 'Am I interrupting something?'

'We've got things to talk about,' said Geary.

'Father and son, of course,' said Blakeney. 'The relationship is obvious. And you've got something to talk about that can't wait till you get home.'

'My father—' David began. He was obviously just about to tell Blakeney that Geary would not be travelling. Geary trod heavily on his toe and spoke to drown the rest of the sentence.

'I haven't seen my son for some time, Blakeney. I need to talk to him quietly. That's why we got on the train early, before it filled up.'

'Strange,' said Blakeney. 'And you with a room at the hotel, too.'

'Blakeney, this is an intrusion.' Geary's heart was pounding. 'I suppose you think your profession gives you an absolute right to pry into people's private lives and listen to their conversations.'

'Well,' said Blakeney, still standing and holding his brief-case by his side, 'some professions do.'

'Just remember that I'm not your . . .' Geary was just about to say 'patient', when he checked himself. Not in front of David! The whole situation was threatening to engulf him. 'Blakeney, please leave me alone with my son,' he said in a calmer tone.

'Certainly,' said Blakeney. Nodding pleasantly to David, he left the compartment.

'He won't have gone far,' said Geary. Once the words had formed themselves, he could not have told whether he had spoken them aloud or merely thought them. He sat back, listening to the drums start up again inside his head and chest. Beside him, David was saying something, but Geary was too confused to take it in. How could he keep David and Blakeney apart? It seemed to him of enormous importance. Not that he knew, specifically, of any damaging information that Blakeney might get from the boy. He simply shrank from the whole idea of his son's being questioned, skilfully, by a specialist in mental disorders who had been set on his track to see if he were insane. For one thing, it might disturb David, arouse the fears that he, Geary, had taken such pains to calm. Among the drums he heard his own voice yelling curses on Philip Robinson. Physically, no sound escaped his lips.

People were beginning to converge on the train. They threaded the corridors, looking busily for seats. All the better, thought Geary. Let the compartment get solidly packed, so that Blakeney would have no chance to come and sit beside David. Above all, let Blakeney continue to assume that he and the boy were travelling together. He would surely make no move to interfere if he thought they were together. The thing was to stay in his seat until the last minute. Leave it till the train was just moving, then jump off.

But Blakeney might come by and see David with an empty seat beside him.

Why should he?

Well, he might go to the lavatory.

It would have to be risked. He could not leave the station and travel down with the boy. The space outside the station was too empty. And there was the problem of what to do at the other end. Suppose there was no train back? Geary clenched his teeth.

'Listen, David,' he said. As he turned to the boy, two middle-aged women came into the compartment and began to load the rack with parcels. 'When you get to the other end,' said Geary in a low, conspiratorial voice, 'I want you to be like a Red Indian.'

'How d'you mean?'

'Watch out for that man. Don't let him see you. When you get on to the platform, hide behind something until you see him leave. He'll probably be looking out for you. But I'm sure you're clever enough to keep out of his way.'

David shrank back in his corner. He looked very small and rather pale. 'What might he *do*, Dad? If he does catch me?'

Geary smiled. 'Every man has enemies, David. The fight between him and me isn't physical. We're not trying to punch each other up or stick knives in each other. But it's a struggle all the same. To put it shortly, he's trying to rob me.'

'To rob you?'

'To take something away that belongs to me.'

'Is it money?' David was struggling to understand.

Geary shook his head. 'That's safely in the bank. It's something else he's trying to rob me of. Something I need very much to keep.'

'Dad, I just don't—'

'Listen, old son,' said Geary. He wondered if the two women were listening. They seemed to be talking to one another. 'Don't bother to try to sort it all out just now. For the time being, just do as I ask you. Keep away from the man we've just seen, and if by any chance he does talk to you, don't tell him a thing.'

A red-nosed old man in country tweeds got into the compartment, closely followed by two men who looked like stockbrokers. Some instinct of protectiveness had made Geary buy a first-class ticket for David, which meant that their compartment had only six seats. The two stockbrokerly men hesitated; they wanted to sit together.

'You take it, Jim,' said one of them. 'I'll go and see if there are two together somewhere.'

'Should be, further down,' said Jim. He sat down beside Geary. 'Come and fetch me, if you find anything.'

'You could let him have your seat,' David whispered.

'There are five minutes yet,' said Geary, also *sotto voce*. 'Let's go on talking till I *have* to get out.' At a normal volume, he went on, 'How are you getting on at school these days?'

'So-so,' said David listlessly.

'Try not to get too bored with it. They can teach you some pretty useful stuff.'

David nodded. He looked disappointed. So much drama, and it had to fizzle out in talk about school!

'What's your favourite subject?' Geary pursued. 'Is it still maths?'

'No. Biology now.'

Looking through the window, Geary saw the big hand of the station clock jump half a minute. How far away was the door? He would have to move fast.

David, struggling to break the silence, came out with, 'Any messages for them at home?'

'Just tell them I hope everything's all right and to ask me for anything they want. Your mother's got an address she can reach me at.'

'What sort of address? The hotel here?'

'A lawyer,' said Geary flatly.

Sidelong, he looked at the boy; so slender, so vulnerable. He had to fight down an impulse to embrace him. Sitting uncomfortably here, among strangers, ready to be whirled sixty-five miles down the line, away from him. . . . How had things come to this pass? He searched his memory for the moment at which it had first become an absolute necessity that he should get away from Elizabeth, from home, from the Institute, from the drums.

'David,' he said in a hoarse undertone, leaning close to the boy, 'I want you to promise me that you won't worry.'

'What about?'

'About anything. But particularly about . . . my being away. You'll find it won't make a scrap of difference, really.'

Hypocrite, the boy's eyes said.

'As soon as I'm settled,' said Geary desperately, 'you can come and stay with me for as long as you like.'

The train jerked and began to move. Alarmed, David cried, 'You'll have to hurry!' Geary started from his seat, took David's hand and gave it a hard, brief clasp, then hurried out of the compartment and down the corridor.

The train was crowded. He chose to move forward because the way back was blocked by a group of youths leaning against the windows and smoking cigarettes. But he had gone hardly a quarter of the way to the door when his path was blocked by the stockbrokerly man, Jim's companion. Perhaps he had found two seats together and was coming back for Jim. Well, now he would not have to trouble and (the thought found a welcome in Geary's hurrying mind) David would be safe from Maurice Blakeney.

The train gathered momentum alarmingly as Geary and Jim's friend dodged each other in the narrow corridor. Jim's friend looked enquiringly annoyed as Geary squeezed past with unmannerly haste. Geary forgave this; after all, the man could hardly realize that he meant to get off the train. They were almost at the end of the platform; would he have to jump down on to the metals? Panting, the drums thundering in his ears, he wrenched open the door and got out on to the step. The last few yards of platform were still flowing by, though the train had now left behind the area normally used by passengers and the space was alarmingly cluttered with trucks, bales and what-not. Was it too late to jump? Geary suppressed the thought and jumped. As he did so he had a sudden vision, fleeting but unmistakable, of the face of Maurice Blakeney. The doctor had come out of his compartment and was standing in the corridor, watching Geary jump off the train.

His mind full of disaster, Geary landed on the platform and was hurled forward on to his hands and knees. Mercifully there was nothing at shin-level, but his head came into painful collision with a wooden crate and for a few seconds he felt half-stunned. Then, slowly, he climbed to his feet. Maurice Blakeney had seen him jump off. His ribs hurt. He hoped David would be safe, neatly tucked in between Jim's friend and the window. He hoped, he feared, he hoped, he feared. But at least he was on the station. He listened: the drums had stopped.

Rubbing his head, Geary turned to go back down the platform and found himself staring straight into a freckled face and deep-set, suspicious eyes he had seen before that day. Of course. The porter, Charley.

'Well,' said Charley, 'what is it this time?' He was carrying a red signal lamp, which he swung gently as if meditating whether to bring it crashing down on Geary's head. 'Doing a bit more study-ing, guv'nor? Working out different ways of chucking yourself off a moving train and breaking your bloody neck?'

'At least,' said Geary, 'you can see it isn't time and motion study.'

'Yes,' said Charley, looking at him narrowly. 'I can see that all right. Getting on a train and then jumping off at the last minute, it looks more like trying to fool somebody or other. Throw them off your scent, like. I tell you what, guv'nor. You're acting like some-body who's running away from the law-er.'

'All right,' said Geary promptly. 'Take me to the nearest police-man and have me identified.'

'Don't try no bluff with me,' said Charley. A slight undertone of uncertainty had come into his voice.

'And don't *you* throw accusations at me,' retorted Geary. All his anxieties and tensions, all the frustrations he had had to suffer that day, turned themselves now into aggression towards Charley. He wished to punish and humiliate this red-haired man in the short jacket. Torn and bruised, he wished to tear and bruise in his turn. 'Come on,' he said brusquely. 'We'll find a policeman and you can repeat what you've just said. That I'm running away from the law.'

'Don't be in such a hurry,' Charley muttered. He backed away, cowed by the malice in Geary's eyes. 'You know as well as I do you've been acting funny.'

'I've been for a short walk on a part of the station that isn't open to the public,' said Geary. 'On being challenged by you and another employee, I left that part of the station peaceably. We'll suppress the fact that I gave both you and him a present in cash. If I was breaking a regulation, so were you. Now as to my jumping off the train. I got off the train because I wasn't travelling. I was seeing somebody off and it started when I was talking and didn't notice the time. That must happen every day. Yet you pick on me and start talking about the law. Well, come along, let's *find* the law.' He gripped Charley's arm. 'I'll tell him you've been pestering me. We'll see who'll come out of it best.'

Charley shook off the hand. His physical strength must have been at least three times Geary's. 'All right, we'll forget it,' he said. 'I don't want to make trouble. If you'd got a good reason for jumping off that train, that's all right, isn't it?'

'Why didn't you ask me the reason?' said Geary. 'Did you think if you threatened me you might get yourself another quid?'

Scowling, Charley walked away and disappeared behind a stack of crates. The triumph lifted Geary's spirits. He walked down the platform to buy himself a drink at the refreshment room. Surely things would be all right. Blakeney would not be able to sit next to David; when they got out of the train, David was sufficiently wary of Blakeney to hide until the coast was clear; disaster had been fended off, perhaps for good. If Blakeney had nothing to report, there would be no case for disturbing him and he would be left snug and safe among the crowds and the impersonality and the friendly, predictable movements of the human tide that swayed about the station.

Warm, reassured, his shoulders touching the shoulders of peaceable strangers on either side, Geary anchored himself like a limpet to the bar, and patiently waited his turn to be served. He felt he had earned a large whisky.

The party, for which Elizabeth Geary had decided not to shorten her skirt, was given by Mr. and Mrs. Marcus Pelt. Adrian Swarthmore kept a careful eye on Marcus Pelt; or, to put a rather finer point on it, regarded Marcus Pelt as a man with whom it was necessary to have an outwardly cordial, if inwardly wary, relationship. Pelt was an economist; a highly successful economist, with a number of influential books to his credit, plus an important university post. He was also a lover of publicity, an indiscriminate lover of it, in any form. He was one of those men of specialized intellect who for some reason find life unliveable unless they have a large and simple-minded audience as well as a small and discerning one.

No medium of publicity was uncongenial to Pelt's restless energy. He was never known to refuse an invitation to appear before the television cameras, dispensing homely wisdom on discussion panels, taking part in quiz contests or even making a fool of himself in parlour games. No newspaper, even the most squalid tabloid, need fear a rebuff when approaching Pelt for a telephoned opinion or for a highly-starred feature article. His dish-like, bespectacled face, always wearing a beaming smile of self-congratulation, looked out at the reader beside each of the articles as it looked out from the shining screen. Marcus Pelt was pleased with himself. He admired the way he handled his life. He was a solid success within his profession and he was also a frothy success with the public. He enjoyed them both, the solidity and the froth.

Adrian Swarthmore, for his part, needed Pelt. The two of them kept up a watchful alliance. Swarthmore was in a position to give Pelt frequent opportunities to advertise himself. Pelt, to do him justice, was a star performer who never let Swarthmore down. Each of them knew, without ever saying it, that when Swarthmore got his big opportunity and grabbed a really central piece of territory on television, he would make more use of Marcus Pelt than ever. And Marcus Pelt, accordingly, would make more use of Adrian Swarthmore. They needed each other, and this need was stronger than their mutual suspicion.

Pelt, standing squarely in the middle of his living-room carpet, looked at his watch and said, 'The first of them will be here soon, Adrian. We'll stick it till everyone's had a chance to bask in your radiance and then light out to somewhere quiet for dinner. Did you remember to book a table, darling?'

Mrs. Pelt, a well-groomed woman who had once been Pelt's secretary, indicated that she had remembered. 'Just for the three of us. At the Pinocchio,' she said.

'Excellent,' said Adrian Swarthmore. Unmarried himself, he approved of the unobtrusive and decorative Mrs. Pelt. 'I'm ready to be devoured by the vultures between now and eight o'clock.'

The Pelts had not mentioned a definite time as a terminal point for the party, so it would do no harm to lay down a limit and make them stick to it. Enough was enough; provincials could be very gruelling. 'Who's coming?' he asked. 'Anybody I know?'

'They all know *you*, Adrian,' Marcus Pelt twinkled. 'But I don't think there's anyone you've actually met.'

'There is, darling,' his secretary-wife corrected him. 'We've asked that woman whose husband has just left her . . . what's her name.' Even she, her voice implied, could not keep track of all these microscopic people.

'Geary,' said Marcus Pelt promptly. 'That chap at the Institute. A quiet researcher with his eyes down on his work. No interest in the wider scene, and, one would have said, no private life. Then suddenly ups and leaves his wife and children. Disappeared into the blue.'

'Is that why you've asked her? To cheer her up?'

'No,' said Pelt. He did not give the sort of party that aimed to cheer people up. 'We asked her because we met her at a dinner-party last week. Your name came up and she spoke of you very warmly. Used to be a colleague of yours when you were just start-ing out in journalism.'

'What's her name?'

'I told you: Geary.'

'No, but her maiden name.'

'I haven't the slightest idea,' said Pelt genially. He considered that he had done enough for this woman by allowing her to come to the party and renew her cherished old acquaintance with Adrian Swarthmore.

There was a ring at the front door. The maid brought in the first arrivals, a couple whose twenty-one-year-old son was just about to graduate from the university and wanted a job in journalism. They had battered down Pelt's defences and more or less invited them-selves to the party. The invitation thus extorted had said nothing about bringing their son, but they had brought him just the same, dragging his gangling form over the threshold and offering it up to Swarthmore with a kind of mute desperation. All three were tongue-tied. Pelt introduced them with a gleam of pure irony, and Swarthmore at once began to talk smoothly and confidently, giving them his entire attention.

'*But you haven't changed,*' Swarthmore insisted.

Elizabeth Geary looked at him with amused affection. 'I hadn't remembered you were such a flatterer, Adrian.'

'You're exactly the girl I remember in 1948,' said Swarthmore. He took a long drink of gin and tonic and put down his empty glass. (Mustn't get drunk: there's plenty that needs watching here.)

'I've lived through the same number of years as you have, since then,' she returned, 'and had my ups and downs, too. A whole marriage, with a beginning, a middle, and,' she shrugged faintly, 'an end.'

'I'm sorry to hear that,' said Adrian Swarthmore gently. He moved closer, protectively, and lowered his voice. 'You must have been through some pain, and the fact that your face doesn't show it—well, it just makes me admire you all the more.'

'And you?' she said, softly pushing the conversation away from a too rigorous bearing-down on her private troubles. 'Have you felt the lure of domesticity yet? Slippers by the fireside?'

'Oh, *no*,' he said dismissively. 'I've been too busy to get married. I don't know whether Miss Right has ever come along—I've never been able to slow down long enough to look closely at her and see. There was always something urgent to attend to.' He sighed, and his face, with those curious mongolian eyes and the full, pronouncing lips, took on a wistful expression.

Elizabeth Geary felt suddenly oppressed and intoxicated by Swarthmore: his closeness, the way he leaned towards her, the burning concentration of his attentiveness. And the energy that radiated from him! Was it sexual? Yes and no; it was generalized, it included sexuality. She realized, with a sting of regret, that she knew very little about such things. Arthur had been passionate enough, but muted; his energy flowed inward. And before Arthur, nothing; a correct upbringing, an efficient career interrupted by a level marriage. Level, then suddenly spilt from under her. She hated Arthur. Never till now; but now, she hated him.

'Now that we've met up again,' Adrian Swarthmore was saying, 'we really must keep in touch.'

He said this to everyone he encountered after a lapse of time. But to Elizabeth Geary it came with the thrust of a genuine offer of relationship. Touch! Would any man *touch* her again? Did she want him to? Yes . . . no . . . a lifetime of good managing, of keeping an even keel, was it enough? Was she satisfied?

But, Adrian Swarthmore! Surely the competition would be too strong altogether? Her mind raced ahead of itself. Well, Angela wanted to move to London. A shake-up would do them all good. Take years off her. For a wild moment, she wished that she had shortened her skirt.

'I'd welcome it,' she said, turning her face up to Swarthmore's. 'As a matter of fact, I feel rather . . . in need of someone to talk to. To advise me. Someone who knows the world.' Oh, how she longed all of a sudden for a man to take her burdens away, to lift them off her shoulders and leave her free to be feminine, feminine, feminine!

Adrian Swarthmore leaned towards Elizabeth and shot a series of quick, roving glances over her shoulder. The party was a wash-out. Nobody there of the slightest interest, except one man who was reported to be an industrialist of considerable wealth, but whose yokel face belied the notion that he could ever have thought fast enough to make half-a-crown. He might have been interesting to talk to: but Marcus Pelt had hold of him, firmly, and Mrs. Pelt was standing nearby to make sure he did not get away and to fend off any intruders.

That left only the assorted horrors, notably the people whose son wanted to be a journalist. He had gone round the whole roster and said a kind word or two to each. There was still half an hour to go before eight o'clock. Elizabeth Geary it must be. And besides . . . at forty, she was still what they called 'a fine woman'. Swarthmore had never been in the habit of refusing any aid and comfort that life threw in his way, and surely life had thrown him some in this instance. She was looking decidedly interested, and if she was recently separated from this husband of hers, then surely it wouldn't take much effort to get her on her hands and knees, begging for it. Rapidly reaching this conclusion, Swarthmore focused his eyes directly on Elizabeth's and gave her a dazzling smile of pure admiration.

'You know, it's a terrible pity I'm tied up for dinner,' he said. 'Would you like to come along and make up the foursome? I've arranged to eat with the Pelts.'

Her face fell. 'Oh, I can't,' she said longingly. 'The children are alone in the house and I don't like to leave them too long. My daughter's fifteen, and she's a sensible girl, but I told her I'd be back at eight and I think that's long enough to leave her.'

'Nonsense,' said Swarthmore. He leaned towards her, coaxing, intimate. 'They'll be perfectly all right. Fifteen? In some countries, girls are married at fifteen and looking after families of their own. Don't be over-protective, Elizabeth.'

'Well . . .' she hesitated. 'I must ring up, then, and if everything's going all right I could tell her I'll be out for an extra hour or so.'

'That's the spirit,' he beamed. 'And I tell you what. We'll have a compromise. You come out to dinner with me and the Pelts, and I'll see that we eat fast and break it up early so that I have time to see you home and have a stirrup-cup by your fireside before I catch the late train back to town.'

She gleamed at him. 'Where's the telephone?'

Buoyant, Adrian Swarthmore floated across the carpet to inform the Pelts that they would be four at dinner. 'I'm sure you don't mind? Elizabeth remembers the old days so clearly, she's filling me in about all sorts of people I've lost touch with.'

'Does that mean we're going to talk about Old Buggins all through dinner?' asked Pelt, who disliked having things sprung on him.

'Not at all, Marcus,' said Swarthmore soothingly. 'All it means is that one corner of the table will be filled up by a charming, rather shy woman who incarnates a bit of my past life.'

'Well, if you put it that way I can't refuse, I suppose.'

The party was obviously running down. People began to come and make their routine thanks to the Pelts, find their coats, and drift out. Adrian Swarthmore ticked them off mentally as he smiled a warm, valedictory smile at each one of them. The couple

whose son wanted to be a journalist made a last desperate attempt
to drive him into a corner and keep him there till he came up with
a definite promise, but he evaded them with contemptuous ease.
Despondent, their loose-jointed son shamefacedly in tow, they
moved away. The room was almost clear: a pleasant evening could
begin.

Then Elizabeth Geary came back into the room, her face hag-
gard with worry. She looked ten years older than when she had
gone out to the telephone.

'I must get home,' she said to Swarthmore. 'I've just spoken to
my daughter and she says my son's missing. He's ten. She says he
hasn't come home. I don't remember seeing him before I came
away, either. I just assumed he was somewhere.'

'I'm sure he was,' said Swarthmore. 'A boy of ten might easily
wander off and come back again. He's probably quite all right.'

'But where would he wander to on a cold winter night? I must
find him. I can't possibly come out to dinner till I—'

'Look,' said Swarthmore. 'Is your car outside?'

'Yes.'

'Well, let me come home with you and help to set this business
straight, and we'll tell the Pelts to go to the restaurant and hold
the table for a bit, and we'll join them as soon as we've located the
boy. He's probably at some friend's house, and the two of them
are playing with a model railway up in the attic and they haven't
noticed the time. I was ten years old once.'

She smiled gratefully, feeling feminine again, but the worry
came back into her face as she said, 'Angela says she's rung up
everyone whose house he might be at. If he's visiting anyone, it's
some new friend we don't know about.'

'And why not?' he shrugged. 'But I can see you'll have no peace
till we've traced him. Let me come home and help. I'll square it
with the Pelts.'

A few moments of explanation followed. Marcus Pelt agreed
with a bad grace to go and wait for them in the restaurant, and
Adrian and Elizabeth were side by side in her car (much-used,
well-kept, inexpensive) and she was driving him home. She managed the car with an efficiency that concealed her inner turmoil.

David missing! Adrian Swarthmore coming home with her! A sense of triumph struggled with a sense of disaster. She still had attractiveness enough to make the great Swarthmore change his plans, inconvenience his hosts, come home with her, her! It had not been necessary to shorten her skirt; she had been right; the charm worked perfectly without that. Parallel to this shining river ran a gloomy ditch full of weeds and mud: had something terrible happened to David? Was she marked out for a series of disasters, was Arthur's leaving her only the beginning, had David been run over or murdered, and if so was it a judgment on her for being self-ish, thinking of pleasure, testing out her womanly attractiveness?

They turned into the drive and stopped: home. Elizabeth Geary switched off the engine; at once, silence and darkness wrapped them round. She tried to move from her seat, but could not. Once she entered the house, anxiety would engulf her like a tidal wave. For the present she was still wrapped in the warmth of her *tête-à-tête* with Adrian Swarthmore; it made her feel secure and protected and she wanted it to last, if only for a moment.

She turned to look at his face. There was just enough light for them to see each other's faces. 'Thank you for helping me,' she said simply.

Swarthmore drew her to him and kissed her. He intended noth-ing more than a comradely salute, but for one tremulous instant she gave her mouth to his with a promise and a surrender that flooded him with sudden excitement. By God, there was some-thing to be cropped here! Then, abruptly, she pulled herself away, a responsible middle-class parent.

Swarthmore, tingling, followed her into the house. It was well-lit, warm, cheerfully furnished, and all these things combined to put up some sort of resistance against the oppressive emptiness of a house whose man has departed. Angela came out of the living-room to meet them. Her long bronze-coloured hair was lustrous in the shaded electric light.

'Well, darling?' Elizabeth Geary asked, her anxiety covered by a shield of briskness. 'Any developments?'

'No,' said Angela. She looked with interest at Swarthmore, who smiled at her over her mother's shoulder.

'Well, we must ring up the police,' said Elizabeth, going into the living-room.

'Now just a minute,' said Swarthmore, following on her heels. 'Number one, I'm going to handle this, with the co-operation of—' he smiled towards Angela—'your daughter, to whom you haven't introduced me.'

'Angela,' said Elizabeth Geary. 'This is Adrian Swarthmore.'

'I knew you were to meet Mr. Swarthmore at the party,' said the girl, impressed, 'but I didn't know he'd be coming back with you.'

'Mr. Swarthmore is here to help us,' said Elizabeth crisply. 'When I rang you and heard about David being missing, he kindly offered to—' suddenly she was shaken by a loud sob that seemed to come from nowhere. It astonished her. She could have sworn that she was nowhere near tears. And indeed, her eyes remained dry. But that single, heavy sob! It indicated that a storm was coming over the horizon.

'Now, listen to me, Elizabeth,' said Swarthmore. His male authority plumed itself in the concentrated female essence of the mature woman and the eager girl. This was living! To hell with Pelt! 'You go into the kitchen and put on an apron and cook chops or scrambled eggs or something while we cope with this. That's the traditional thing for mothers to do at times of stress, and I think it's the right thing. When we get him back, he'll want something to eat, and it'll be as well to have it ready. So off you go. We'll come and tell you when we find him.' Protectively, tenderly, he hustled her out, then turned back to the daughter.

'We won't telephone the police, Angela,' he said, 'till we've tried all the obvious things. First of all, what's your brother's name?'

'David.'

'David. And he's ten, your mother says.' His eyes narrowed in concentration, so that they looked almost Mongol above the high cheek-bones. (On camera!) 'Old enough to go quite long distances on his own, if he's a mind to. Any friends who might have him for the evening?'

'I've rung up all the ones I can think of. If he is in someone's house, it must be someone I don't know.'

'Is that likely?'

She shook her head.

'Well,' he said, 'that leaves the police and the hospitals. I think we'll start with the hospitals first. They'll give a simple Yes or No to an enquiry, whereas the police, once they get hold of a thing . . .' Leaving the sentence unfinished, he picked up the telephone book. The hiss of frying came from the kitchen. He was king of the house! Adrian Imperator!

He was just asking the first hospital whether they had admitted a ten-year-old boy that evening when Elizabeth's voice reached his ears with 'Da-vid!' on a high, astonished note. The boy had come in through the back door, perhaps hoping to avoid notice, and run slap into his obediently cooking, aproned mother.

'Thank you, it doesn't matter,' Adrian Swarthmore said to the nurse at the other end of the line. 'The young rascal's turned up.' He pitched his voice in a genial, confident key: mustn't make heavy weather of this. Boys will be boys. The fright would be just enough to flutter her heart, butter it with gratitude, soften it, make his task easier, Adrian the bold.

Was he slightly drunk? He put the receiver down, turned and caught Angela looking at him, watchful and shining.

'Well,' he said, breathing easily, 'that's that. He's home.'

She smiled, and as he smiled back he looked deeply into her eyes, giving her his full attention.

All through the journey, David had sat very still beside Jim and Jim's friend. The two shopping women had talked incessantly, their voices not quite loud enough to be consistently audible above the rumble of the train, and David had found that to keep his attention fixed on their talk, trying to catch what they were saying, kept him occupied and took his mind off the two things he wanted, for the time being, to forget: the melancholy problem of his father and the terrifying problem of his father's enemy.

He kept his mind away from these two worries because neither of them appeared to be soluble. David was a thoughtful and well-balanced boy. He had inherited the thoughtfulness from his father and the balance from his mother. Both qualities co-operated to give him the solid common sense that refuses to beat its head against the brick wall of a problem that will not yield. How could he, a boy of ten, influence his father to behave more normally? He was not convinced by his father's outward show of reasonableness; he had welcomed it mainly because it showed a willingness to keep up appearances, to go quietly dotty instead of openly running mad. Again, how could he stand up against this smooth-faced fat man with his sinister rimless glasses? The man was not only an adult, with an adult's physical strength; he was also a well-dressed man who looked prosperous and authoritative; the sort of man who could get railway officials or policemen to see his point of view and obey his instructions, whose word would always be taken against a boy's.

Being ten years old was a bore. It was hampering and humiliating. Listening hard to the two women, David went on thinking in some unreachable corner of his mind, and his chief thought was that he must grow up. There was something called adolescence. He heard his mother talk about it, and occasionally saw the word in print. Adolescence was when you were a teenager. Adolescents were supposed to have problems, but on the other hand these problems could not be worse than the problems he already had, and it would be a relief to be, as it were, officially equipped with problems: to have problems that were acknowledged and talked about. If you were an adolescent, like Angela, people looked at you sympathetically and wondered, while being too polite to ask, how you were getting on with your problems. Whereas, if you were ten years old, they just looked over your head and assumed that you couldn't have any problems and that schooldays were the happiest days of your life.

Thirteen, David thought, was the target. Get to be thirteen, tall and strong, with hair down below and real problems, and everything would be better. But would his father last that long? Could he rely on still knowing his father in three years' time? Would he come to his senses, get off the station, and live a normal life? Or would he get worse and worse until one day he ran screaming mad along the platform? And if so, whose fault would it be? Had Mother driven him mad? Surely not, she was always quiet and reasonable. Angela? Just a silly girl who couldn't do anything as *big* as drive a person mad. He? Never. Who, then?

Suddenly David saw a vision of Dr. Blakeney's bland, hairless face. His father's enemy. Trying to steal something from him. All at once David knew what this man was trying to steal—had, in fact, stolen. His father's sanity.

Thirteen. When that magic birthday came, he would be tall and strong. He would exercise every morning, put on muscle, ready for the day. Because whether or not his father lasted long enough, David was going to get that man with the rimless glasses, to get him, to fix him. Revenge. You drove my father mad, screaming among the porters. Tie him up. Take that, and that. A bull-whip. You thought you'd get away with it, that everyone had forgotten. One person hadn't forgotten. Thirteen. My problems are important, more important than any grownup's. He saw boys of thirteen, fourteen, right on to eighteen, at school. Mad on girls. Whistling at them from bicycles. Or passing books round. What sort of books? Anything that had a girl-smell. An explosion of laughter when one huge lad showed something out of his pocket. A sheath. What was that? Something for girls. Problems that people worried about, helped you, not things you had to carry in silence. When the ticket collector came David silently showed his ticket, but inwardly he was screaming, 'My father's mad on the station back there; look out for the man with the rimless glasses, he's killing my father but I know about it, I'll get him.'

When I'm thirteen, he reflected soberly, putting the ticket back in his pocket, I'll tie him up and flog him. He won't dare tell the police because he'll know he sent my father to the mental hospital. Long, shiny wards. I'll visit him. Dad, I flogged him. Looking at me like an animal. Then, suddenly, his eyes show that he understands. You made the score even, son. I'm proud of you.

The train slowed. People began to stir, to collect belongings, to rise from their seats. This was it. He must avoid the enemy, remain invisible but watchful. His father had entrusted him with a sacred task, and, mad or sane, it was his father he was fighting for. As the long, lighted platform slid into sight, David scrambled over the toes of Jim and Jim's friend and hurried down the corridor to be first at the exit. There was, of course, a risk in this. Rimless might make for the same exit. So he went down the length of the next coach. This put him rather far down at the rear of the train, which was good. It would give him a long view down the platform. He wanted to be certain of watching Rimless leave the station.

For David had a plan. Revenge was at least three years distant, but there was no reason why he should wait three years before beginning to act. Rimless must be kept under close observation. David's veins filled with a dark, secret exultation as he thought of the careful assembling of information, the detailed note-taking, the building-up of a complete picture of the enemy's habits. But one thing was essential. He must know the man's name and where he lived. Perhaps his father could give him these facts, but David felt a deep instinctive preference for working on his own. He felt protective towards his father, and he wanted his father to know nothing of this, nothing at all until the day when he could go to him and say, *Justice is done. You are avenged.*

He jumped down from the train and walked stealthily forward towards the ticket barrier. Everyone had to pass here. Hiding behind a truck loaded with crates, he peered cautiously out. The first few passengers, walking quickly to beat the rush, were already streaming past the ticket collector. Rimless was not among them. He must be just about getting off the train: looking about for him, perhaps. David felt a delicious thrill of danger. His plan was bold, and for its boldness it deserved to succeed. He wanted to wait until his father's enemy passed through the ticket barrier, then slip out and shadow him to the taxi-rank. It was obvious that such a man would not go and stand at the bus-stop with the common herd. He would take a taxi. And David wanted to hear what address he gave to the taxi-driver. He was determined to be within earshot at that moment.

He watched, then froze. Maurice Blakeney was coming down the platform with a long, loping stride, his briefcase hanging slackly by his side. His face was directly towards David, and for a terrifying instant he seemed to be staring straight at him. But the eyes were unfocused, the thoughts elsewhere. He came up to the ticket-collector, turned so as to present his profile to the watching boy, and waited his turn among the slowly shuffling crowd.

In an instant, David was out of cover and wriggling in among the press of bodies just behind Maurice Blakeney. By good luck there was an immensely large young man just to the rear of the doctor, a giant who overtopped him and also stretched out beyond him on either side. In the lee of this behemoth, David was as well hidden as behind a barn door. He waited, holding his ticket in a damp hand, as they shuffled towards the exit. Rimless was through, a sharp-elbowed old lady was through, then the giant was through, then David was through. He slipped like an eel among the shadows. Rimless was in the taxi-queue. There were half a dozen before him, and only two taxis in sight. As David watched, another taxi drove up, circled, and came nosing in to the queue. Then another, then another. Rimless was next but one: no, the two in front of him were together, he was next. The other taxis drove away. The station forecourt was empty. David shrank back against the wall; a cold wind had sprung up, and he shivered. With one eye he checked the escape route: if Rimless turned and saw him now, he could always run. But it would spoil everything; it would put the plan back years. God, let him not turn round. God must feel as he felt when he fed the ducks. Don't throw the next crust this way. I'll be good, I'll pray hard in church, I'll believe.

A taxi drove up, wheeled, stopped in front of Blakeney. Blakeney moved forward and opened the door. The people behind moved automatically to fill the space left empty, but before they could do so David had darted in, on Blakeney's heels, and was standing behind the taxi as if about to open the boot. First watchful, then nimble, then immobile, he suggested the kind of half-starved child who hung about Victorian railway stations rather than a well-fed modern boy. People turned in surprise to look at him. The driver craned.

'Is the boy with you?' he demanded.

'Boy?' said Blakeney. He turned and followed the driver's eyes. All he saw was a small, blue-coated figure slipping away round the side of the taxi and moving rapidly, at the risk of his life, across the road. There was no traffic. The figure reached the darkness at the other side, and disappeared.

'With me?' said Dr. Blakeney. 'No, not with me,' and he climbed into the taxi and gave his address. His mind was preoccupied with the business of the day, and especially with a paper he had agreed to deliver on some complex questions of psychological interpretation. That boy? Some child from one of the local back streets, playing round the station? Or could it have been Geary's boy? He blamed himself for not looking out more determinedly. Perhaps the boy needed help. Geary had jumped off the train; he had seen that. So the boy must have travelled alone. Really he ought to have gone and found him. He was not nearly old enough to be wandering about in the dark by himself. Supposing it was Geary's boy, what was he doing, skulking round the side of his taxi? Had he come up to ask to be taken home, and failed to muster the nerve at the last minute?

Putting aside all other thoughts, Maurice Blakeney gave his full attention, as the taxi sped towards his home, to the problem of Geary's boy. He was a kindly man, and now he felt a definite sense of guilt that he had spent the journey in making notes for his lecture, and not made a definite search for the boy after he had seen his father jump recklessly off the train. 'We're all too busy,' he muttered, self-accusingly. 'A duty, a human duty! We've all got too much work to do.'

The taxi drew up outside his house, and as he paid the driver Maurice Blakeney said pleasantly, 'I wonder if you'd do something for me.'

'What is it?' asked the taxi-driver, carefully preserving his spotless discourtesy and unwillingness to oblige.

'You'll be going back to the station, won't you?'

'I'm on a station licence,' said the driver pityingly.

'Well, you remember that boy who was hanging about? The one you wanted to know if he was with me?'

'Yes.'

'Well, keep a look-out, and if you see him again, try to get hold of him and take him home. I think he may be lost. If you do take him home, his parents—his mother will pay you all right.'

'I got my hands pretty full,' said the driver. 'You think there's a child lost, you want to ring the police, that's what they're for.'

Dr. Blakeney silently handed him his fare plus an enormous tip.

'All right, sir,' said the driver. 'If I see him. Course, I can't get out of my cab. I'll just have to look round.'

'That's right,' said Maurice Blakeney. 'Just look round.'

The taxi drove off and he went into the house.

David ran until he was certain of not being pursued. Then, his heart pounding, he halted under a street lamp. Failure! The campaign against Rimless had started with an abysmal failure. The man would have recognized him, for sure. He would be on his guard now. On his guard! Against what? He was perfectly secure. David did not even know, had no idea, where to get hold of him, and if he simply relied on running into him by chance, the odds were that he would never set eyes on him again. And this was the big scheme! This was how you revenged your father, who had been driven mad by a scheming cheat with rimless glasses!

Leaning against the street-lamp, he thought hard. Name, address. His father had called the man by his name, he remembered that distinctly, but the name itself would not come back. He had been too flustered and frightened to retain it. Well, that must stop. Steely courage, unshakeable nerve, coolness, in future!

Think, think . . . the name. 'Blogshaw, leave me alone with my son. Flakeshift, leave me alone with my son. Bruno, leave me alone with my son.'

Gone. In fact, never come. The beating of his frightened heart had deafened his ears. In disgust, David heaved his shoulders away from the lamp-post and began to walk. He went down one mean street, then another. There seemed to be no main roads here. He stopped, to find out whether his ears could catch the rumble of traffic that would lead him to a main road he might recognize. Silence; the night seemed to have swallowed up all activity. Pondering, discouraged, David walked on and on between the silent rows of houses. Some of them showed the blue glare of television in the front room. Others seemed deserted. Only from one came any human sound: a piano and people laughing and singing. He felt desperately lonely, but unwilling to go home. He would find no cure for his loneliness there.

How long had he walked? The chill November air seemed to have reached the inside of his bones. What to do, what to do? Some help must come.

He turned another corner and it came. A patch of light, people loitering, a warm, fatty smell: ah, fish and chips! Suddenly he was ravenous, and the money his father had given him was rich and heavy in his pockets. Feeling adult and adventurous, he went in and bought a large portion, swathed in newspaper, and walked along the street eating fish and chips, and feeling better. A person to be reckoned with: able to take care of himself.

'Bindweed, leave me alone with my son. Blakeney, leave me alone with . . .' *Blakeney!* David almost whooped for joy. Bolting the last of the chips, throwing away the empty ball of newspaper, he quickened his pace.

To find the station, to get home . . . suddenly, it was simple. He would ask the next person he saw. He did so. Directions, easy to follow. 'You're out late, sonny, by yourself.' He smiled tolerantly. 'I'm going straight home, now.' Guarded, poised. Don't tell them anything. All he had to do was get into the house, sneak up the stairs, and make out that he'd been reading in his room. He rehearsed it. But Angela looked for you! She came up to your room! Angela must be blind. She must have looked straight at me and not seen me. Lies. Never mind. It was his right to go and see his father, and if he could only claim that right by lying, he would lie.

The station. A taxi. As he went up to it, David's heart gave a wild lurch. This was the same one that had taken Blakeney! He recognized the chequered band round the top of the doors, he recognized the driver's trilby hat and suspicious eyes. Too late.

'Oh, it's you, young feller-me-lad. A fare I had earlier on, he told me to look out for you. Said you were lost or something.'

'I'm not lost,' said David. 'I'm on my way home now.' He gave his address. 'Can you take me?'

'The man said your mother'd pay the fare.'

'I'll pay it myself,' said David. 'I've got some money specially.'

The driver, satisfied, nodded and they slid forward. David's mind was racing. How could he get the driver to tell him where Blakeney lived?

'That was Mr. Blakeney who asked about me, wasn't it?'

'Was it?' said the driver, smoking.

'He's my uncle. Only I've forgotten where he lives.'

'Well, if he's your uncle,' said the driver indifferently, 'you can ask your mother and she'll tell you.'

'I don't think she knows,' said David, timidly persistent.

'You got problems in your family,' said the driver. He drew up outside David's house. 'Here you are. Nine bob.'

The correct fare was six shillings, but the driver surmised, correctly, that David had never ridden in a taxi by himself before, and had not heard of the custom of tipping. With prices what they were, a man had to take care of himself. He gave David two sixpences change for a ten-shilling note and drove away.

David moved into the shadow of the hedge. The normal number of lights seemed to be on in the house. It couldn't be very late. His adventures had taken some time: an hour? More? It couldn't be much after eight. He crept round to the back door. Go in through the kitchen. Nobody would be cooking at this time.

He was wrong, and his mother met him with a blast of oven-heated air and a cry of surprise.

David stood still. The first thought to occur to him was that his mother looked different. Her face looked thinner and younger, with a high colour that was different from the colour she got from the heat of the gas-stove. Even her voice, when she uttered his name in that glad, bitter, complaining cry, had a different tone. He could not have put words to it, but he knew, as they stood there looking into one another's faces, that his mother was slightly altered from the woman he had last seen at breakfast that morning.

Then Angela came into the kitchen, stepping accusingly, and behind her came a man with glasses and high cheek-bones, looking curious.

David closed the door behind him. He knew now that everything was changed, both in his mind and outside it. He had been to see his father: that had opened a chapter that would go on writing itself, now, whatever he did. And he had come back to find his mother looking different, Angela stepping into the kitchen like a white hunter moving through elephant country, and this man here. The whole feel of the house had changed. He could tell at once.

'Where've you been?' Elizabeth Geary almost whimpered. She had not yet recovered her self-command; did not, indeed, know where to look for it.

'Why, am I late?' David asked. He was obeying his first impulse, which was to brazen it out. But immediately he wished he had not. The foolish piece of countering gave his mother the opening she needed. It allowed her to unleash the easy floods of anger and reproach.

'Now, David, you've caused us all a lot of anxiety' (us! ALL!) 'staying out *hours* later than you've ever stayed out before, and without a *word* to anybody. If you've got some good reason why we should have been driven wild with worry, you'd better say what it is, but if you're just going to be *silly . . .*'

'How about coming into the sitting-room?' said Adrian Swarthmore, looking over Elizabeth's shoulder and taking command. 'Scenes that develop in the kitchen are always the worst. Let's all go and sit down in comfort and straighten things out. I'm sure David didn't mean to cause any anxiety.'

Oh, you're sure of that, are you? David resented this man fiercely. Who did he think he was? What had he been doing to the household while he was away? His father must be rescued. This smoothly domineering man must *not* take over his authority.

The ham rashers that Elizabeth was cooking under the grill began to scorch. Blue smoke filtered to everyone's nostrils.

'Oh, dear, I'd better attend to this.'

'Let David tell me his story,' suggested Adrian Swarthmore. 'David, we haven't met, but I'm an old friend of your mother's from before you were born, and if you'd like to tell me what you've been doing that's kept you out so late, I'll try and make it all right with her.'

He smiled, confidence-inspiring, and David at once decided that he was a worse enemy than Blakeney. The drama of life! Enemies springing up everywhere! The thought gave him a kind of happiness.

Swarthmore led the way. David lingered for a moment.

'Shall I tell him, mother?'

'Yes, dear,' she said, bending over the food. 'I feel I've got to pull myself together. Just give Mr. Swarthmore the facts and then have some supper with us. Whatever you've been doing, I expect you're hungry.'

'No,' he said proudly. 'I've had some fish and chips.'

'Fish and *chips*?' She straightened abruptly. 'Who's been feeding you?'

'No one. I bought them from a fish-and-chip shop.'

'And ate them,' she said bitterly, 'from a newspaper in your hand, walking along the street. And knowing all the time that I was worrying myself sick. What makes you so *cruel*?'

'I didn't do it to be cruel.'

'David!' called Swarthmore, putting a little iron into his voice to make the boy realize that he must be obeyed.

'Go in,' Elizabeth said, her face hard and strange to David. 'Get your confession over before I come in with the food.'

David went into the sitting-room. Swarthmore was in an arm-chair, his father's armchair, and Angela was standing behind the sofa, her hands resting on its back, like a prosecuting counsel.

'Sit down, David,' said Swarthmore. 'Now look, we mustn't make a big fuss over all this. You've done a silly thing, but we all do silly things now and again.' He smiled.

'I haven't done a silly thing,' said David.

Swarthmore's lips tightened. 'What kind of thing have you done, then? How would you describe it?'

'I've been to see my father,' said David.

Swarthmore looked guarded. This was a development he had been unprepared for. Before he could speak, Angela was asking David, furiously, 'Where?'

'In London,' said David.

'You went all the way to London by *yourself*?'

'I had to. If I'd asked anyone to take me, they wouldn't have.'

Angela looked at him closely, full of doubt as to whether he could be telling the truth. 'But how did you know where to find him?'

'Find who?' asked Elizabeth Geary, who was feeling

stronger now and had come in with a tray because she was getting inquisitive.

'He says he's been to see Daddy.'

Elizabeth sagged. She wished she had not come in. The kitchen, so rashly deserted, now seemed a haven of blessed unconsciousness.

'How can he have?' She turned to David. 'What is all this?'

'I've been to see my father,' said David.

Inside him, a savage pride welled up. They were united against him. They were together, and he was on the outside. This home, these women, had changed in a few short hours. The man was something to do with it. The man's presence was the cement that walled up the minds of his mother and sister against him. Very well. He would use any club that was heavy enough to knock the walls to pieces. And what club was as heavy as the truth?

'David,' said Elizabeth Geary, 'if you're telling the truth, go on.'

'There's nothing much to go on with,' he said. 'I've been to see my father, that's where I've been all day, and he's all right and we had lunch together, and he gave me some money, and when I got back I went and had some fish and chips and then I came home in a taxi.' His recital filled him with wonder: I did all that!

'Why don't you sit down, David?' Swarthmore put in. He had had time to recover himself, and had decided that all-embracing compassion was the line most likely to bring him through unharmed. 'Let's talk quietly about it.'

'I am talking quietly.'

'Suppose you did go to see your father,' said Swarthmore, controlling himself, 'there's surely no harm in that. You miss him, don't you?'

Fury travelled across David's heart as fast as a crack across a mirror. His feelings about his father were private feelings. Not even God could pry into them, and certainly not this man with the soft, insolent face who was sitting in his father's armchair. He stood silent, glowering.

'David,' said Elizabeth Geary, helplessly, 'I don't know where your father is. And if I don't know, how do you?'

David whirled to face her. At that moment, he had no pity.

He hated his mother. He would willingly have ordered her to be flogged, and Angela with her.

'They're talking about him,' he said. 'Boys at school are talking about him because they hear their parents talking about him. He spends all his time on Paddington station. He won't leave it for anything. He lives in the hotel and he spends all day sitting on the station.'

'David, however did you get hold of such a *ridiculous*—'

'It's not ridiculous. It's true.'

'But your father's the last man in the *world* to do anything like that.'

'How do you know?' said David brutally.

'David,' said Swarthmore. He felt he must intervene. 'Are you perfectly sure that the boy, or boys, who told you this weren't just pulling your leg?'

'Yes, I'm sure.'

'Was it a friend who told you or an enemy?'

'It was a boy called Julian Robinson who told me, but it doesn't matter whether he's a friend or an enemy. I've been there, today, and I've seen him and it's true.'

Elizabeth Geary had been holding the tray. Now she put it down helplessly. 'Did he tell you himself that he never leaves the station? Did he tell you—' she gestured her helplessness—'anything about what he's doing?'

'They're saying he's mad,' said David. He had not meant to speak loudly, but his voice came out loud in spite of him. 'They say he can't leave the station, he's got something the matter with his mind that makes him go mad if he leaves the station, so he never will leave it, except to be taken away to a . . . to an asylum or something.' As he reached the word 'asylum' David began to cry. He sank down in a chair and gave all his attention to crying. His weeping was not loud, but it was terrifying in its thick, strangled intensity.

His mother went to him, but he pulled away, and her arms, that would have offered him shelter, fell to her sides. She looked appealingly at Swarthmore, but though he realized that the time had come to do something he had no idea what to do. As the two adults flickered in indecision, it was Angela who spoke. Unnoticed, she had been seething with anger, which now came spilling out.

'Isn't it just like David to believe some silly story he's picked up at school from some absolutely foolish *child*, and then come back and burst into tears all over everyone?'

'Hush, Angela. Don't be unkind.'

'I like that. *Unkind*. What's David being?'

What she meant was that David was spoiling something important. This electric evening, the arrival of Swarthmore with his face that millions recognized, switched on and beaming *for her*, the touch of drama in the air, her mother's sexual interest in this new male, which Angela knew nothing of and would have been shocked to hear about, but which entered the air like the scent of a tropical flower which she could not help breathing—all this was an important step forward in her advancing life, an adventure, an initiation, something she both needed and claimed as a right after the dreary years of childhood: and now David, who had been a uniting absence, was suddenly a dampening presence. His part in her drama was to get into some really serious trouble, not to be drowned or run over, she did not ask for his death, but to make some satisfying display of desperation, to run away from home and be traced with difficulty by the police, half-starved under a hedge.

'David's worse than unkind,' she said. 'Behaving like a silly crying *child*.' This was still the most cutting word in her vocabulary. After it, speech failed her. She tossed her head and went striding, colt-like, out of the room.

'David,' said Swarthmore, carefully keeping his voice gentle, 'don't you think it would be a good idea if you went up to bed? You could get some rest while your mother and I talk over what you've told us.'

Hate conquered David's grief. What right had this man to talk over his father's plight? With anyone, much less his mother?

He stopped crying and looked up accusingly at Swarthmore. 'Are you staying?'

Swarthmore gave him an easy smile. 'Don't worry. I'm only here for the evening. I'll be going back to London soon.'

'Oh, *don't* go,' said Elizabeth Geary suddenly.

Her utterance surprised them all, herself as much as anyone. It was pure impulse. The words seemed to jump out of her throat. Until they did so, she had no idea how much she wanted Swarthmore to stay and protect her, how much she dreaded the moment when he would go and the house would be manless again.

'David,' she said, to cover her confusion, 'you go up to bed and I'll come and bring you some nice hot milk. Don't worry, darling. It's all very upsetting for you, everything that's happening, but it'll come right.'

'That's what Dad said,' he told her sullenly. But he got up from the sofa and took himself off, with no backward glance at Swarthmore. She could not find it in her heart to chide him for this rudeness. Suddenly, his vulnerability seemed to her greater than her own.

'Now,' said Swarthmore, glad that the situation had shifted back on to a manageable level with the removal of the children. 'Let's get a grip on all this. First of all, I'm hungry.'

'I'll feed you,' she said. Her face and voice were empty; she felt drained of personality, able only to function. And indeed clever Swarthmore, emperor of women, had divined this. Let her move, fetch food, minister to him, while blood slowly came back into her channels. Her problem was a real one, and he was willing to help her, but he could do nothing until she responded to him. He wanted to help her and also to claim her, possess her, make her helpless, leave her smeared and spent and trembling, his woman: and the two objectives were stuck together and would not come apart in his mind.

Elizabeth put ham and eggs before Swarthmore, excused herself—her throat was too tight to eat—and went upstairs with some hot milk for David. He was already in a deep sleep. Or was he pretending? She set down the milk and bent close. No, it was true sleep. He must have tumbled into it, with some sound protective instinct, as soon as his head touched the pillow. Fleeing from consciousness, fleeing from the thorns that surrounded him into the green thicket of dreams. Angela was stirring angrily in her room. Elizabeth decided not to face her. In her depleted state, she would

have nothing to give. She closed David's door quietly and went
downstairs to Adrian Swarthmore.

He turned quickly to face her, his expression open, honest,
uncomplicated. 'Elizabeth, have you got a spare room here that I
could sleep in tonight?'

'Yes,' she said. She felt as if a prayer had been answered.

'Are you going to eat?' he went on, ticking off necessary prelimi-
naries before getting down to business.

'I'm not going to. I'll have a cup of tea,' she said.

'Good. Let's both have one. But before you go out to boil the
kettle, tell me who I can ring up to check on this story about your
husband.'

'Do we have to check on it?'

'Certainly. Because if it's true, you're the one who'll have to do
something about it.'

'I suppose so,' she said. 'But I feel so dead about it all. I'd far
rather just let it go and do nothing.'

'I know you would, Elizabeth, but look at it this way. If he's
really had some kind of nervous collapse, that explains why he
was such a fool as to leave you. The situation of a woman whose
husband leaves her is always a wretched one. But if he's mentally
ill, if he needs attention in a hospital, that lets the woman out. The
break-up *can't* be her fault.'

'Perhaps,' she said, 'they'll go about saying I *drove* him mad.'

'Take it a stage further. Suppose you want to divorce him. If
he's mad that's going to be no trouble.'

'But why bring me into it? Either he's mad or he isn't mad, and
if he is it'll soon be discovered and he'll be put away.'

'I don't agree. It needn't be soon at all. He might go on for
months, quietly off his head, and as long as he behaves normally on
the outside, not making disturbances or shouting in public places,
this could drag on until he runs out of money and gets thrown
out of his hotel. And meanwhile everybody's talking behind their
hands. Think what young David must be going through at school.
It must be pretty average hell if it drives him to get on a train and
go to Paddington all by himself.'

'Julian Robinson,' said Elizabeth, her voice still heavy and indifferent. 'His parents are Philip and Jennifer Robinson.' She always remembered names. 'You'll find them in the telephone book. If you want to ring them, do it now, while I'm in the kitchen. I'm quite a strong person, but I can't take any more tonight.'

'You won't have to,' he told her gravely. 'That's what I'm staying for.'

She threw him a look of pure gratitude through the curtain of her fatigue, and went off to the kitchen. As soon as she was gone, Swarthmore leafed rapidly through the telephone book. This was pure gold. Wait till he told Ben. What a leader for an actuality series. Well-known scientist (if he wasn't well-known he soon would be) takes to living on Paddington Station. The lonely man who came back from the frontiers of knowledge. Or, put it another way: where is humanity going? Well-known scientist at home only among the journeying.

He might be just plain nuts. But the interview it would make!

'Hello?'

'Am I addressing Mr. Philip Robinson, please?'

'Speaking.'

'Mr. Robinson, you don't know me, but my name is Adrian Swarthmore.'

'Oh?' Robinson didn't watch television much, thought he had heard the name somewhere, but . . .

'And perhaps I can indicate the nature of my business if I tell you that I'm ringing from the house of Mrs. Elizabeth Geary.'

'Elizabeth Geary?' Robinson's mind positioned itself rapidly, like a compass needle swinging round. 'Arthur Geary's wife?'

'Precisely. Arthur Geary's wife. She's a very worried woman, Mr. Robinson.'

'And you want to ask me something about Arthur Geary?'

'Correct. Mrs. Geary has been seriously disturbed by certain strange rumours. I'm an old friend of hers and I want to give her any help I can, and spare her the distress of making enquiries herself. Would you mind telling me anything you know relating to Arthur Geary's present condition and whereabouts?'

He wished he had a tape recorder on the telephone. But you couldn't have everything.

Robinson briefly told what he knew and ended by reveal-ing that he had mentioned the matter to Dr. Maurice Blakeney. Swarthmore had to be told who Blakeney was, but once he knew, he broke in with a dismissive shower of thanks for Robinson's helpfulness. He could not get off the line fast enough so as to dial Dr. Blakeney's number.

Blakeney was relaxing after dinner, smoking a cigar. He came to the telephone reluctantly. When he heard what Swarthmore wanted, he at once became professional, guarded.

'Yes, I know the man you mean. I was asked quite unofficially if I'd take a look at him. There was no question of a profes-sional diagnosis, of course. It was just that some friend of his, an ex-colleague—'

'Philip Robinson,' said Swarthmore, checking details.

'Ah, I see you know. Yes, Robinson had some story about meet-ing Geary on Paddington Station. Said he was in a strange state, and would I look at him. So I had a few minutes' chat with him this morning, at the hotel. I've been expecting Robinson to ring and ask me what happened, but he hasn't yet.'

'I'm ringing instead,' said Swarthmore. 'I'm an old friend of Elizabeth Geary's and I'm helping her over this.'

'Elizabeth Geary? The wife? I see. Well, I haven't got much to tell you. Couldn't have, under the circumstances. The man's cer-tainly showing signs of strain. I saw that straight away, when I met him this morning. His defences are too close-knit. He's taking too much care not to show that anything upsets him; he must be very upset somewhere inside. It doesn't take a specialist to see that. Then I saw him again this afternoon. Whether he ever goes off the station I can't say, but he was certainly there this morning and again at about four this afternoon. He had his son with him. Did the boy get home all right, by the way?'

'You saw them together?' Swarthmore asked. He was excited at this new scent. 'How was Geary acting?'

'His guard was much more down, of course, when he was with the boy, and he caught sight of me unexpectedly and it rattled him. Shook him so badly he couldn't be polite to me.'

Behind him, Swarthmore heard Elizabeth come in with the

tea-tray. Never mind, she would just have to be in on this. He couldn't stop now.

'Why was that, do you think?' he asked, tightening his grip on the telephone as if afraid someone might wrest it from him. 'Why did it shake him so much to see you?'

'He's got a fairly evident horror of being checked up on. Guilt feelings, perhaps, about leaving his wife and children. Or it may be something deeper. Just what, I couldn't say without spending more time with him.'

'Is that a possibility?'

'Probably not,' said Blakeney. 'I only do what people ask me to do, and no one's asked me to take on Geary as a patient. I should say that if his condition declines he might well find himself in a mental hospital, and then he'll be taken care of by the appropriate—'

'D'you think it will decline?'

'I simply can't say.'

'And if it doesn't? If he just stays as he is?'

'He won't stay as he is,' said Blakeney with bleak finality. 'He'll get better or he'll get worse. And it may be that the thing to do is simply to leave him alone. I certainly shouldn't feel like intervening.'

'It's very worrying, you know, for his family and friends.'

'If his family and friends are worried,' said Blakeney in a slightly haughty, my-dear-man voice, 'they can always hire somebody to stick close to him and see that he doesn't throw himself off the platform. Beyond that, at the moment, I don't think it would be right to go. People often get into a nervous state, you know, and then straighten up and come out of it without needing any outside help. The mind can throw off a mild infection just as the body can. And that's much the best way.'

'Thank you, Dr. Blakeney,' said Swarthmore. 'It's very good of you to have taken the trouble. I can assure you it's most appreciated.'

They politely bade each other good-bye. Swarthmore put down the receiver.

'A mild infection of the mind,' he said, half to himself.

'What was all that?' Elizabeth asked. She bent over the tea she was pouring so as to hide her trouble and fear.

'It seems this chap Philip Robinson, whose son has been so charming to David, took it upon himself to telephone a certain Dr. Maurice Blakeney.'

'He's head of the Grayson.' She was seriously frightened now.

'My dear girl, don't panic at the mention of the Grayson,' said Swarthmore. 'Robinson just asked the man to look into Arthur's situation and see if he seemed to be acting strangely. So he did and his verdict is that there's nothing to be alarmed about.'

'It's all very well for him to say that. Doctors get very callous.'

'His opinion is likely to be right, nevertheless.'

'David said it was true he was mad,' she half-wept, half-spoke.

'David? A ten-year-old boy whose emotions are deeply woven into the pattern?'

'Adrian,' she begged, 'what shall I do?'

'First,' he said, 'come here.' They sat on the sofa. He took her hand. 'Elizabeth, I'm going to see you through this.' And get you to bed, he thought. You'll be a first-rate bit of fun after all that frustration. 'Arthur's on Paddington Station. The doc's opinion is that he can be left there without coming to any harm, as long as he's watched.'

She nodded. 'But who's going to watch him?'

'I am. I'll do part of it myself and the rest I'll have done by other people.'

'Oh, please, Adrian, don't involve a lot of other people in this.'

'I didn't say a lot of other people. I have one or two trusted minions, who are as silent as the grave. And if the job gets really big I'll hire someone from one of the old-established, very discreet private investigation firms. In any case, nothing will leak out and nobody will be offended or annoyed. The object being, simply, to look after Arthur and stop him from doing any harm to himself. Until—'

'Until when?'

He turned to face her. 'Dr. Blakeney says he'll either get better or get worse. A pretty fair prediction about anybody who's ill. If he gets better, well, he leaves the station and fits himself back into society, we all breathe a sigh of relief and the episode's closed.'

Like hell it is. Not until he's done me a bit of good with Ben. 'If he gets worse, well, we needn't plan that in detail now.'

'But what *shall* we do if he gets worse?'

'Elizabeth, the trying time for you is *now*. If, which God forbid and which I don't seriously anticipate, your husband turns out to be seriously deranged, he'll be looked after like any other ill person. In any case, it'll be out of your hands and mine. It's just at present, while everyone's waiting to see which way the cat will jump, that you need all your patience and strength.'

'And it's now,' she said, softly, 'that some power sent you into my life to help me.'

'Yes,' he laughed. 'A power named Pelt.' He jumped up. 'Good God! I'd forgotten him!'

A quick flurry of page-turning to find the number of the restaurant, a request to speak to Dr. Pelt, a wait while Dr. Pelt was called from his table, then a grave, hushed, confidential explanation: quite impossible to leave her in the lurch. A very difficult situation here. Sure you would understand. Anything you want to discuss? . . . What about a date in town? Wednesday next? Perfect. He came back, careless and confident, Pelt disposed of.

'Now, Elizabeth,' he said—ah, the quiet ease with which one speaks to an old friend, a true friend!—'tell me your real feelings about all this.'

'All this?'

'About your husband, his desertion of you, his *villeggiatura* at the station, the rumours that he might be mad, the effect on your children and yourself, any and every one of those. Talk about it.'

'I'm not a Catholic, Adrian,' she said, 'and if I were, you're not my father confessor.'

He was glad to find that she still had some fight left.

'All the same, I want to be told things,' he insisted. 'I want to see the situation from the inside. I care what happens to you.'

'Why should you, Adrian?'

'Because I used to like you very much and then life took you away from me, and now life's brought you back to me and you're in trouble.'

'In other words, you're sorry for me as you might be for some old charwoman with rheumatics and a hard-luck story.'

'Elizabeth, don't be bitter. People love you for yourself. If they want to help you, it's because you're worth helping.'

'Oh, Adrian,' she smiled through a mist, 'I want so much to believe that.'

'I give you permission to believe it. It's true.'

'What am I going to do with my children, Adrian?'

'Let them ride it out. They have their own stability. At any time now the girl will become absorbed in the attentions of boys and that will keep her mind off everything else until she gets married. After that she'll have her own worries. And David—'

'It's David I'm worried about. Why did he go to see Arthur today without saying a word to me?'

'Easy. He thought if he did say anything you wouldn't let him go. He might have felt obscurely that you'd be jealous of him for setting up some sort of relationship with his father when you hadn't any.' He paused, and looked at her keenly. 'Would he be right, Elizabeth?'

She shook her head slowly. 'Deep inside me, I've already accepted that the story of me and Arthur is over. I know he won't come back.'

'Why are you so sure?'

'Because for five years at least we've been going more and more deeply into our separate burrows. I hardly knew him towards the end.'

'Was that anyone's fault?'

'I can't say. He seemed to be off somewhere where I couldn't touch him. Perhaps if I'd been a different person I could have done. He could never talk about his work and that made him lonely. I think that was the beginning of it.'

'Why couldn't he talk about his work? It was too abstruse?'

'It was too abstruse for ordinary people, and if he did meet anyone who could have understood what he was doing, he couldn't tell them. He was inhibited.'

'By anything in particular?'

'Just after the war,' she said, 'he was working on something that

was covered by the Official Secrets Act. He wasn't allowed to discuss his work except with a few colleagues, and then behind closed
doors. Well, one day, in about nineteen fifty-one it must have been,
he came to me and said that the Official Secrets ban no longer
applied to him, that he'd changed his line of research and switched
to something that he could tell people about if he wanted to. But
somehow, he never did.'

'Had he any close friends?'

'He used to be very close to his elder brother. But he went out to
New Zealand and Arthur hasn't seen him for ten years. He's often
talked of going out there for Christmas or something, but when
it's come to the point we've never felt that the expense would be
justified.'

'Anyone else?'

'He had a very close friend he'd been at college with, called
Geoffrey Winters. But Geoffrey died about three years ago.'

'Under sad circumstances?'

'They thought he killed himself,' she said.

Both were silent, thinking of Arthur Geary as he paced the
draughty platforms and remembered his dead friend. His friendship had not been a cable strong enough to bind Geoffrey to the
earth. He had broken free and been snatched up into the windy
sky. After that Arthur had given up friendship.

'Is he fond of the children?'

'Very, I think. Of course they're not as close to him now as they
were when they were little things. But David always will be close
to him, I should say.'

A cool, hard mood descended on Adrian Swarthmore. Well,
Geary, old man, you're going to be of some use to one person at
least. Your station escapade is going to provide me with the story
I want, the blockbuster that will put me right with Ben. And by
clearing out and leaving your still very attractive wife, you've set
her up nice and warm for me.

He turned to her. 'Be happy, Elizabeth. Life isn't over for you.
These troubles—they'll go. Think of yourself a bit—indulge yourself now and then.' He drew her close, meaning to kiss her, but at
that moment Angela's footstep was heard coming down the stairs.

'Mummy,' she said, poking her head accusingly round the door, 'I'm going out.'

'Oh, no, dear! At this hour?'

'Just to Hazel's,' she frowned.

'But walking about the streets alone, at this hour!'

'Let her go,' urged Swarthmore in a low voice.

'Why on earth, darling,' Elizabeth asked, struggling for command, 'do you want to go and disturb Hazel at this hour when she's probably in bed?'

Angela laughed shortly. 'Hazel never goes to bed till *midnight* at least. She stays up in her room, reading and playing records. She's got all the most marvellous records that I can't afford to buy. She *likes* me to drop in on her then.'

'But,' said Elizabeth helplessly.

'Look, Mummy, you know where Hazel lives. It's about two streets away.'

'You go, Angela,' said Swarthmore, nodding. 'It'll do you good to get out a bit.'

'How can you—' Elizabeth turned on him with a flash of real anger. But Angela had chosen to accept his authority, withdrawn her head, and was gone. The front door closed.

'Don't treat me like nobody in my own house, Adrian,' said Elizabeth.

'I'm not,' said Swarthmore, impenitent. 'I'm treating you like somebody. A very special somebody. I thought it would be nice if Angela went out for a bit. Nice for us, I mean.'

She stood up. 'And in order to get me to yourself, you're prepared to let a girl of fifteen wander about all over town by herself in the middle of the night?'

'Sit down,' he said, pulling at her. 'Two streets isn't all over town.'

He caught her hand, but she broke free, running to the door. He heard her step in the hallway, and then the sound of the front door opening.

'Angela!' Elizabeth's voice called into the raw night. 'Angela! Come back at once, please!'

She was just in time. The girl had reached the garden gate, and in another few seconds would have been swallowed up in the darkness. There, she would have heard her mother's voice and walked steadfastly away from it, her heart being at that moment very hard. But her mother's authority was too much when it went with a seeing eye. She could not disobey with Elizabeth's gaze full on her.

Her hand fell from the latch of the gate; she paused; she turned and came back. Only her eyes, studiously averted from the eyes of her mother, spoke of the frozen anger inside her.

Elizabeth allowed the girl to pass in silence, then shut the door and enclosed them both in the warmed and lighted air of the house, its reasonableness and safety.

'That's right, darling,' she said cheerfully. 'I'm sorry I had to call you back, but I never said you could go in the first place, and if you want to talk to Hazel it would be much better if you rang her up.'

Angela went along the hallway, her back towards her mother, as if she had not heard. When she got to the bottom of the stairs, she turned, one hand on the banister, and said, 'I'm going to bed.'

'Come in and say goodnight to Mr. Swarthmore, then,' said Elizabeth, keeping her voice bright.

Angela shot her a look of contempt. (It's war between us, and you still want me to keep up the decencies!) Without speaking, she turned and went on up the stairs.

Elizabeth went quickly into the living-room, her heels clicking on the oak tiles. She was angry, yes indeed! Swarthmore had offered to help, to support, to liberate her feelings by removing them from the squeezing vice of tension. So, naturally, she had admitted him, laid herself open. And now look what he had done! Tried to supplant her!

Swarthmore got to his feet as she came in. He was uncertain what to do. Soft-talk her? Or go ahead with the rough stuff and trust it to crack her right down the middle?

'Elizabeth, there's no need—'

'I don't think, Adrian,' she said, 'that there's much point in going on with our big scene. The mood's rather broken, wouldn't you say?'

'Shattered,' he said wryly.

'Just as well, perhaps. It seemed to be taking a wrong turn, somehow. I think when you came to the house you genuinely came as a friend, to help me. Then the idea came to you that the lonely, helpless, deserted wife wouldn't be averse to having a pass made at her if you could get the daughter out of the way.'

'Just forget that, Elizabeth,' he said, fighting back. 'Forget that you ever said it or ever thought it.' His eyes, full of an easily-summoned sincerity, held hers for a long moment.

'All right,' she said at last, 'We'll cut the last four lines out of the record. And don't think I'm not grateful, Adrian.'

She went off, nevertheless, to get his room ready. Their scene was, as she had decreed, over. Swarthmore paced the room, found some whisky and soda, angrily knocked back a stiff one. High and mighty bitch! Closed, all cracks plastered over! No wonder she had driven her husband mad. But then he had probably been no better. Withdrawn, aloof. He felt a hot animosity for both of them. Why did the fool of a woman refuse an opportunity to have a little fun? Who did she think she was saving it for, anyway? Did she think, at her age, that the men were going to stand in line?

It would serve her right if he gave her copper-haired daughter a bloody good knocking-up.

That was as may be. Meanwhile, Arthur Geary was on Paddington Station and the cameras of Consolidated Television were going to follow him there.

Elizabeth came back to say his room was ready. He thanked her, and they said goodnight and smiled at each other like old friends, but as he lay down in the spare bed, wearing a pair of Arthur Geary's pyjamas, the room was furry with his hate.

Then night folded over the house. Each in a separate brick-and-plaster compartment, a forcing-house for dreams and anxieties, all four sank into an uneasy sleep. The young girl and the man were angry, though in different ways and about different things. The woman was bewildered, pierced by thin needles of longing: her needs were acute and contradictory. She wanted to be possessed and dominated, but also to be left alone, and also to be invested with authority, and also to be loved and pitied. Her ills were no longer curable; her life was over. The boy, for his part, was immersed in simple dismay.

Because dismay can rise to the surface of the deepest sleep, dragging its sufferer with it, David woke soon after midnight. His mind, instantly lit by the full beam of consciousness, threw up one huge, shocking fact. His father was hurt. His ribs were broken. Lying in the dark, David relived the moment when his father had suddenly peeled off his shirt and vest and showed him that grey wall of plaster round his body. Thinking of it, he could picture the broken staves of bone inside. Sad, sad. His father's body. The body which had given him life, when his father had done that to his mother and made him into something living like frog-spawn. And now the two bodies were separated, their heat quenched, and his father was alone, comfortless on a strange bed and with his ribs broken.

A fall down a flight of steps? His father had never been a clumsy man. A banana skin? Was it likely? He must have been shielding him. There were enemies. Blakeney's face, wearing a disdainful smile, rose before David's mind. Enemies strong enough and unscrupulous enough to attack his father, to break his bones, to destroy him.

Weeping, David rose quietly from his bed and went across the landing to his mother's room. Elizabeth Geary was asleep in the bed she had shared with Arthur Geary. When he was little he used to creep in beside them sometimes, when the darkness began to encircle him with shapes of fear. He would go quietly into their bed and lie down with his back touching whichever one happened to be on that side. Then the fear would go away and he would sleep.

Now he was bigger, he never did that. The fear in the nursery darkness had gone away, but other fears had come and this time it was for ever; they would never go away and he would have to live with them. He was ready for that. What drove him to his mother's softly-sleeping form was not fear now, it was sadness. The sadness of their loneliness and of his father's broken body.

Elizabeth Geary awoke as David moved in close to her. For a

wild instant she stiffened, ready to defend her body against viola-
tion. Something in her, not her mind but some part of her nervous
organization too primitive to come near language, signalled that it
might be the man she had wrongly trusted who was breaking in
on her sleep. Within a second she knew it was David and sank back
into maternal drowsiness.

'What is it, darling? What is it?'

He burrowed.

'Darling, you're crying. Never mind, darling, oh, never mind.'

Her paved surface was broken, her efficiency not even a
memory, and she hugged him frankly in her lonely bed.

David tried to form words. He wanted to tell her that Dad was
hurt, that he had enemies who had cruelly broken his ribs, that
the hospital had put a band of plaster round him and he walked
everywhere now with the plaster making him sweat and itch.
But when her arms went round him, something switched off the
terrible dismay inside his mind, and he sank promptly into sleep.

In the guest-room, Swarthmore stirred irritably on his pillow,
his sleeping face a mask of ill-will.

When the alarm clock went off beside Elizabeth Geary's bed at
seven-thirty, David was still beside her and the two of them were
sleeping heavily. Elizabeth Geary woke up with the sense that
something was wrong. Her mind knew that it was worried before
it could remember what it was worried about. Then she remembered. Adrian Swarthmore was in the house and had to be coped
with in addition to all the other things she had to cope with first
thing in the morning.

She got out of bed and gathered up her clothes to take them to
the bathroom. David stirred and woke.

'Hullo,' he said shyly. Now that daylight had come, it made him
shy to find himself in his mother's bed.

'Hullo, darling,' said Elizabeth with cool tenderness. She made
no reference to his having come to her bed.

'Is it time to get up?' he asked.

'You can stay in bed and wake up slowly,' she said. 'I'm going to have my bath and get dressed and then the bathroom will be free and you can do the same.'

She went to the door, carrying her clothes, then stopped, turned back, and got her dressing-gown and put it on. Normally she walked along the landing in her nightdress, but this morning was different. Swarthmore.

Lightly as she moved, he heard her footstep go past his door. He was lying on his back, arms folded behind his head. The pale light lay softly on the pepper-and-salt stubble on his jowls.

There she goes, the bitch, he thought. Damned inconvenient to wake up here instead of in town. Got to waste half the morning in the train.

Then he remembered that the train would come in to Paddington Station. His prey. Geary. Must get a look at him. Lying on his back, Adrian Swarthmore began thinking. His brain became ice-cold, precise, turning over silently and with immense power. Fresh morning air circulated about the room; he felt well. Things were going to jump his way.

He got out of bed and went over to the mirror to comb his hair, examine the whites of his eyes, check on the increasing proportion of salt to pepper in his stubble, and generally survey his appearance. Not bad. He was not old yet. Physical vigour welled up inside his chest. He heard the sound of water-pipes in the next room, and imagined Elizabeth Geary's naked body in the bath, but without disturbance. So that one had slipped away: well, there were plenty more, and plenty better. He was going to the very top, where they were all to be had for the picking. He wasn't at the very top yet; better admit that frankly. High up, but not at the top. It would take a successful television series to put him right up there, and that meant impressing Ben Warble, and that meant getting a scoop, and a scoop meant Geary. So Geary was the target, and he was the rifleman. It was as simple as that.

Elizabeth Geary padded back. Then he heard the boy run along to the bathroom and splash a bit, then run back. A few minutes later the boy knocked on the door and came in, clothed, with a cup of tea for him. Always the decencies. Always the little middle-class decencies of hospitality. If I had raped her on the hearthrug,

Swarthmore reflected, sipping the tea, I'd still have got a cup of tea and a lift to the station.

The boy had told him the bathroom was free. Putting down his empty cup, he opened the door and went out on to the landing. Over his pyjamas he was wearing a thin dressing-gown of Geary's. In the bathroom he washed and cleaned his teeth with a new, cellophane-wrapped toothbrush that Elizabeth Geary had put out. The decencies again. The unexpected overnight guest should not come down to breakfast with the acid discharge of twenty-four hours on his molars. But there was no razor. Geary had taken his with him and Elizabeth, unlike many women, did not shave.

His clothes were back in the room. Naked, he gathered up his, or rather Geary's pyjamas and put on Geary's dressing-gown. He could not be bothered to put the pyjamas on. The gown would cover his nakedness for the few seconds it took to get back to his room, and besides, there was nobody about.

He opened the door. Angela Geary, her dressing-gown held tightly about her and her face still steeped in drowsiness, was coming down the corridor. Adrian Swarthmore stood quite still and let her come right up to him. Suddenly he felt lecherous. He wanted this fresh young feminine thing close to him. With an openness that surprised him, he relished the fact that his manhood was veiled from her sight by nothing more than a thin, lightweight dressing-gown. He felt coarsely commanding.

'Ah, good morning,' he said softly. He knew that she could see the pyjamas under his arm, that she was confused by his nearness and his maleness.

'Good morning,' she said, meeting his eyes quickly and then looking away. Her voice was not quite a child's.

'All calm after the storms of last night,' he said to her confidingly. 'Order restored, eh?'

'Thanks to you,' she said shyly. Her shyness excited him. He longed to sink his teeth into her, to ruffle her, to scrub her white skin with his stubble.

Seeing that he made no move to stand aside and let her get into the bathroom, the girl turned to go back to her room. But before she had completed the action, he had slid out of her way and in at his door, chuckling an apology.

'Sorry. I'm not awake yet.'

I was never more awake in my life, he thought, throwing away the dressing-gown. Well, if it isn't her it'll have to be another one. And soon.

He dressed quickly. The captain, the king, the man who makes things happen. The stiff coating on his chin and cheeks only made him seem more masculine, more earthy. Stand aside, I've waited long enough. Oh, I've done all right. But I'm not going to stop short of the top, the very top, the pinnacle. Within twelve months, he promised himself, you'll have everything you want, *everything*.

Downstairs, the boy was finishing his breakfast. Elizabeth was gracious as she put half a grapefruit in front of Swarthmore and went off to boil him an egg. She had decided to forget his clumsiness. He grinned into his half grapefruit. The boy excused himself politely and said he had to be off to school.

Elizabeth returned with the egg. Angela came down and joined them, and they all sat like well-behaved strangers. Angela, dressed now as a schoolgirl, kept her face averted and spoke only to her mother. Swarthmore, eating, watched her covertly. He must not let her go too far into her shell. He needed her. Presently, Elizabeth left the room and Swarthmore seized his opportunity quickly, for Angela seemed about to follow her.

'Angela,' he said in the same confiding tone he had used upstairs, but without its brazen sexual undertone, 'have you got a photograph of your father anywhere?'

She looked up, her face full of quick interest. 'Yes. Upstairs.'

'You see,' he said, 'I know your mother's worried about him and I want to see if there's anything I can do.'

She nodded, still watching his face. It's all right, he thought. I didn't frighten her away.

'But I must know what he looks like,' he explained.

'Mummy took down all the photographs,' she said, glancing towards the door. 'I suppose she didn't want to be upset. But I had one up in my room and I've kept it there. You can borrow it.'

'It'll be enough if I just look at it. You say it's in your room?'

'I'll bring it down,' she said, and hurried out.

He waited. Elizabeth did not come back; in a moment he heard her seeing David off, and then she went upstairs. Angela must have passed her on the stairs, because she came in immediately afterwards. Her face had a lovely glow of excitement.

'Here's the picture,' she said. It was a good, clear one, about nine inches square, in a light frame. Swarthmore studied it intently.

'Is this a recent one?'

'Two or three years. He hasn't changed. At any rate,' she added, 'he hadn't when I last saw him and that was only a few weeks ago.'

She paused as if about to confide in Swarthmore or ask him something. Swarthmore waited, his eyes on the portrait. But she said nothing more, and in a moment Elizabeth came in and asked him when he wanted to go to the station.

'And you must go to school, Angela,' she said. 'I know it isn't far, but you're due there in about ten minutes and I expect they want you to set an example now that you're a prefect.'

'Oh, a *prefect*,' said Angela, her voice full of quiet loathing of the stupid, unchallenging world of childhood and school. Swarthmore felt that this was for his benefit and that it said a great deal. He gave her a warm, understanding smile. God knows there was not much chance of getting at her now, but perhaps in a year or two he would meet her in London, without her mother, and then it would be a different matter. Tenderly, he watched her go out of the room. My little golden pheasant. Sit on your nest a little longer.

As the high steel arches of the station came into sight, the train slowed, but the beat of Adrian Swarthmore's heart became faster. He leaned forward in his seat. He was riding in a first-class carriage and the seat had comfortable padded arms. As he put his hands on the arms he noticed that the palms were slightly damp. He was making a present of a little of his sweat, free of charge, to British Railways.

Swarthmore had a corner seat, and as he looked out, round the edge of the tastefully gathered-in curtain (first-class compartments only), he could see long dreary streets which slanted diagonally away into a smoky, bricked-in distance. Ant's-eye view. The swarming, stopped-up life of the Londoner. He thought of the station ahead, its curious doubleness. At one level, the epitome of London: urban, crowded, for ever anchored by steel bands in its grimy setting. On another, weightless, floating, a place of transit to other places. And to one man, a refuge.

He closed his eyes for a moment in order to summon up his memory of the photograph. Geary's oval, serious face. Deep-set eyes, a rather wide mouth. Shoulders that looked broad. He had forgotten to ask Angela whether her father was tall or short. With that breadth of shoulder, he was probably about medium height. Otherwise he would be an exceptionally big man, and the girl would have said so.

Platforms and luggage wagons glided backwards past him, quickly, then slowly. The train stopped. His fellow-passengers stood up and shuffled, tightly packed, towards the exit. Adrian Swarthmore stayed in his seat, his damp palms resting on the padded arms. Now that the moment had come, he felt tense. It was no light thing to hunt a man in order to mount his head above your fireplace.

Among the last passengers, Swarthmore got out. He hurried down the platform, eyes down, fearful of being recognized. He felt an instinct to take cover while he worked out his next move. The licensed buffet was nearby: he decided to have a drink, then suddenly remembered that he was still unshaven and decided to go to the station barber first. Sitting in the barber's chair, feeling the light scrape of the blade cutting swathes in the rich lather, he felt proud of his self-command in not going for a drink immediately. They would have been open. They opened at eleven o'clock.

Shaved, his face tingling, Swarthmore came up the steps from the barber's shop. He was now on Platform One, and another licensed buffet was a few steps away. He decided to get a cup of coffee and a miniature-sized bottle of brandy, and pour the brandy into the coffee. Fired by the beauty of this resolve, he pushed quickly into the refreshment room. He bought the brandy first, so that the coffee should not go cold. Then he went to the coffee-machine, ordered a cup, and watched it poured out. As the cup filled, he fingered the small brandy-bottle in his pocket. He felt cold and empty and unnerved. But it would all be all right in a minute. He would carry his cup over to a corner table and tip the brandy in and drink it. The coffee would warm his stomach and clear his head and the brandy would course through his veins and put iron into his nerves. Then he turned his head and saw Geary.

'A shilling,' said the woman behind the counter. She pushed the coffee towards Adrian Swarthmore and smiled encouragingly. He stared uncomprehendingly at the cup for an instant. Geary was sitting at a table only two or three yards away. There was an empty cup beside him and he was reading one of the non-illustrated weekly papers.

Swarthmore put down a two-shilling piece and moved away with his coffee. The woman called after him, 'A shilling change, sir!' Swarthmore halted and the attention of the people nearest him was caught by the tiny incident. Several of them, including Geary, looked up at him.

Swarthmore, his face burning, went back and collected his change. When he turned again to go and find a table, he saw that Geary was still looking at him. There was something like a gleam of recognition in Geary's eyes. Swarthmore hurried past with his face averted. He felt utterly disorganized. His plan had been to look round and identify Geary at his leisure, then, under cover of a stranger's anonymity, stand or sit near to him, even to engage him in casual talk. He had taken it absolutely for granted that Geary would not recognize him. His face was well known to many people, but not, on the whole, to people like Geary.

Now he felt hunted. His stomach fluttered with longing for the coffee, but he set it down and walked straight out through the door. He could not have sat down to drink it under Geary's eye. Whether Geary knew who he was or not, Geary had seen and marked him. Outside, he moved fast until he was safely in the shadow of the booking hall.

Another refreshment room? More coffee? His overstretched nerves revolted at the thought of going through the performance again. Taking the miniature bottle from his pocket, he unscrewed it and put it to his lips. Half? No, all. He tilted his head back hungrily. A passer-by threw him a pitying glance, as if he were a meths drinker on the Thames Embankment.

Breathing deeply, Swarthmore dropped the empty bottle into a litter-basket. The brandy raced through his nerve-centres. He stood beside a row of telephones, Adrian the hunter. The wild lion Geary was in his den on Platform One. A single narrow escape must not shake the marksman's nerve. He moved cautiously in the shelter afforded by the blank side of the bookstall.

Unconcerned, walking with an easy swing, Geary came down the platform, passed the bookstall, saw Swarthmore, and stopped. His face wore a pleasant smile.

'Excuse me,' he said. 'But I believe I know you. It's Mr. Swarthmore, isn't it?'

'Yes.'

'We haven't met, I know,' said Geary. 'But I believe you're an old acquaintance of my wife's.'

The brandy sang in Swarthmore's nerves. He nodded, watching Geary's eyes.

'I saw you on television once. In some panel discussion. I'd been out and I came in to find my wife watching it and she pointed you out. She said you used to work together in Manchester.'

'Yes. Just after the war.'

'I hadn't met her then, of course,' Geary smiled. His mind was easy. The station was really working for him this morning. He felt safe, sheltered, willing to pass the time of day with anyone. Also, he wondered if he had disconcerted Swarthmore by staring at him in the refreshment room. 'I expect you're used to people recognizing you,' he said.

Swarthmore felt panic rising in his chest. He, the hunter, was being driven into a corner. He must find some way of counter-attacking. Strength: be brutal.

'I was visiting your wife last night, as a matter of fact,' he said heavily.

'Oh,' said Geary. 'You came in on the eleven o'clock train, I suppose.'

The perfect cover-up, Swarthmore thought. Oh, I congratulate you, boy. Aloud he said, 'Yes. It's very convenient.'

'She'll have told you all about it, of course,' said Geary. The zest had gone out of his face, but beyond that he did not seem much disturbed.

'Yes. I was sorry, naturally.'

'Naturally,' said Geary. 'Well, pleasant to have met you.' He inclined his head slightly in a vestigial bow, and moved away. He had, under the circumstances, no wish to chat with Swarthmore. He carried the scent of old sorrows on him, and besides, Geary did not, at close quarters, like the look of the man.

Swarthmore watched as Geary walked away down the platform. One thing, at least, was clear to him: Geary was indeed spending all his time on the station. He moved about it in the way a man moves about his own garden. Most people, on a railway station, are either hurrying or loitering. Geary was moving naturally. He had time to stop and talk, yet no compulsion to drag the talk out so as to kill time. For a moment, Swarthmore wondered whether Geary had not, after all, found the secret of happiness. Then he pulled himself together. The hunter is permitted, fleetingly, to envy the lion. But he is not permitted to let the lion escape with his life.

He went back into the refreshment room, which was now safe from Geary. Another coffee and brandy? No! he felt full and warmed, but still nervous. He ordered a chilled glass of lager, and sat down to drink it and think calmly.

Three evenings later, Swarthmore was in his flat, talking into the telephone. His living-room had soft lighting and big windows, and because the central heating was very good he often kept the curtains open on a cold night and looked out. Tonight, as he talked, he kept raising his eyes and looking at the river far below and the tall buildings on the opposite bank. His flat was high up, and the sky looked very cold. But the air inside the flat was warm, the light was soft and the carpets were thick. It was the kind of contrast Swarthmore enjoyed and constantly sought after.

As he talked, however, his enjoyment drained away and he became anxious and irritable.

'Are you sure? Aren't any of them available?'

'No, I'm sorry,' said the girl at the other end. 'They work as a team and they're all out on an assignment.'

'But Sir Ben himself gave me his assurance that they'd be available.'

'Well,' she said reasonably, 'it's tomorrow you want them for, isn't it? They'll be available then. They're all going to report at nine-thirty.'

'It's just that I had a specific arrangement,' Swarthmore grated, 'to get them round to my place this evening for a briefing. This job tomorrow is going to be a very delicate one, and at the same time a chance to make television history. It's important to me to work with a crew who understand the nature of what we're doing. I explained all this to Sir Ben and it was his suggestion that I should get them all in here and give them a drink and get some kind of *rapport* with them.'

'I'm sorry, Mr. Swarthmore. I mean, I quite see that, but our orders are that a crew has to stand by to be at the disposal of the *Showcase* people if they want it.'

'And of course, being the night I needed them, the *Showcase* people did want them,' said Swarthmore softly.

'They're all at the airport. All those African ministers are going home.'

'African ministers,' said Swarthmore and rang off. Sitting quite still, he looked down at the dark river and that other coiling river of headlights beside it. The sky looked cold enough to kill a bird. He imagined the camera crew shivering in their overcoats on the airport tarmac. He hated the men who ran *Showcase*, a highly popular programme of news and background. In particular, he hated the man who was its chief. This man had that uncanny streak of instinct that he, Swarthmore, had never been able to discover in himself, though he claimed to have it and was sick with longing for it, or rather for the power that would come to him if he could develop this streak and turn it to account. It was power he longed for, power, power.

'So my camera crew will turn up unbriefed, sleepy-eyed, cold, disgruntled and probably with incipient pneumonia,' he said aloud. 'And then, if we make a mess of it, I'll have to explain to Ben that it was all my fault.'

The sound of his own voice, falling heavily among the solid furniture, made him feel lonely. Abruptly, he drew the curtain and sat down in front of the electric fire. There were several ways in which he might divert himself during what remained of the evening, and he gave his mind to the business of choosing one of them.

When Swarthmore stepped out of his taxi at the Consolidated studios the next morning, the sky overhead was as white and thick as china clay. The driver saw him looking up at it as he fumbled for the coins to pay the fare.

'Yes, we shall get it, sir,' he said, jerking his thumb upward and grinning wryly.

'Get what?'

'Snow,' said the driver with dour satisfaction. He pocketed the money and drove off.

Swarthmore cursed as he walked over to the reception building where the camera crew would be waiting. With everybody in a filthy temper already, it only needed a snowstorm. He pushed open the door of the room in which the crew had been told to assemble. Three anonymous-looking young men, in thick jerseys and narrow trousers, looked up at him with faint hostility, cupping cigarettes in their hands.

'Are you the crew?'

'Some of it. The chief hasn't arrived yet.'

'Yes, he has,' said a flat Northern voice behind Swarthmore. The chief cameraman, a stocky man with a bald head and heavy glasses, was just coming in at the door. 'Didn't get to bed till two o'clock. I wouldn't do it to a dog.' He shuddered in his belted overcoat.

'Never mind,' said Swarthmore easily, masking his own bitterness. 'I've got a nice easy assignment for you today. No moving about. We just stay on Paddington Station.'

'Paddington Station?' asked the chief cameraman incredulously. 'What are we doing? Taking engine numbers?'

'We're doing an interview,' said Swarthmore, keeping his voice smooth and professional. 'With a man who doesn't know he's being interviewed.'

'Candid camera stuff?' asked one of the anonymous youths, looking up.

'No. Something more subtle. It's a character-sketch really,' said Swarthmore. 'The man we're after is an eccentric scientist. He lives on Paddington Station. Never goes off it.'

'Where does he put his test-tubes?' asked the chief cameraman.

'I know nothing about how he manages his life or his work,' said Swarthmore, controlling himself. 'Our object is to explore the man's nature. To get a picture of his life. Above all to find out why he never moves away from the station.'

'He's daft, that's all it is,' said the chief cameraman. 'He's off his trolley.'

'If he's mad,' Swarthmore conceded gracefully, 'he's mad in an interesting way because he's an interesting man. What we're going to do is to take a look at him and if possible talk to him. Now it may be difficult. I hope you'll accept it as an exciting challenge to your powers.'

'Holy God,' said the chief cameraman, looking round at his subordinates as if inviting them to share his amazement.

'It may not be possible,' Swarthmore went on, 'to get an ortho-dox television interview with him. If he saw the cameras he'd simply walk away, I'm pretty certain of that. So we shall need a lot of telescopic work. Get a number of shots of him walking about the platforms and so on. Then, when we've got a fair amount of material, I'll try to get him into conversation. I'll use this.' He showed them a tiny tape-recorder with a microphone that could be hidden behind a flower in the button-hole.

'You can get better ones than that,' said one of the young men. 'You can get transistor radios that keep playing all the time and when you get it home you clean off the sound of the radio and play back the tape.'

'Yes, very wonderful, I'm sure,' said Swarthmore. 'And you'll tell me next that I look the sort of person who'd walk about on a big London station with a transistor radio blaring away in my hand.' He annihilated the youth with a cold stare, and proceeded. 'If the worst comes to the worst, and it probably will, we can use telescopic shots entirely and fit the tapes to them in one way or another. I'll be welding the shots together with a commentary in any case. There'll be a lot of editing, but you won't be concerned with that. Once we've got a can full of telescopic material we'll just bring it back here and I'll edit it with the producer.'

'All right,' said the chief cameraman, who had not taken his overcoat off. 'Let's get started then. I could do with a short day today. It's my belief I'm coming down with something.'

They went outside and got into the van. As they drove off, the first flakes of snow began to fall.

Geary saw the snow as he was dressing. He had felt pleasantly lazy that morning and had treated himself to breakfast in bed. After eating, he lay back and stretched luxuriously, then opened the newspaper which had come up with his breakfast tray, and read contentedly for some time. The newspaper told him its daily renewed tale of strife and anguish, and also warned him that England was seriously threatened as a great power, even as the kind of second-class great power she had been since the Second World War. Geary took this news calmly. The warmth of the bed was pleasant and it occurred to him that bed would still be as warm and delicious even if England became a very poor country indeed.

At last he got out of bed, turned on the hot tap, shaved and washed. Then he put on his clothes. It was while he was buttoning his shirt that he saw the snow. Pleased, he stepped quickly over to the window. His room was at the side of the hotel and did not overlook the station, but he could see roofs, a street with pavements, and people and traffic. The snow was just beginning to form a white powder on those surfaces where it was undisturbed. Even underfoot, it had not yet been trodden into a brown paste: it was white with dark, damp-looking holes where people had walked, and long dark lines where cars had been driven.

Geary felt exhilarated by the snow. It broke the monotony of his life at the station, not only by altering the appearance of everything, but also by bringing about a subtle alteration in the tempo of life. People walked differently when they walked through snow; they looked up at the sky in a different way when they were wondering whether it would go on snowing or not. With a pleasant sense that today was going to be unusual, Geary finished dressing, took his overcoat and went down to the station.

As he came out of the hotel Swarthmore saw him at once. The camera crew were having coffee in the refreshment room and Swarthmore was sitting on one of the benches in the station foyer, pretending to read a newspaper. Geary strolled comfortably past, wearing his overcoat and a dark felt hat, and went to the newsstand, where he chose with deliberation a couple of magazines. Then, putting the magazines in his pocket, he walked down the length of the platform till he reached the point where the giant glass roof ended and the open sky began.

Swarthmore ran to the refreshment room and gathered his team. He pointed down the length of the platform to where Geary stood with his back to them, contemplating the snow. There were not many people about on the platform, and Geary, as he stood motionless before a curtain of falling snowflakes, looked like a man meditating in an almost deserted building: a strange, gaunt cathedral, perhaps. The chief cameraman at once set up one of the cameras and began filming.

Up at his end of the platform, Geary stood peacefully watching the snow forming a light layer on the curved roofs of freight wagons, on the tops of walls, and on the roofs of buildings that overlooked the station. It was sticking, but how easily it stuck depended on the nature of the surface it landed on. On the railway lines, for instance, the snow had already covered the metals, turning them into magical lines of whiteness that threw up light into the leaden sky. It had also covered the sleepers. But the cindery surface of the ground underneath the sleepers was not yet covered. It was merely speckled with snow. Here and there, at the foot of a wall beside the lines, there was a patch of ragged grass, and these patches had absorbed the snow between the grass-blades so that they still showed as dark.

As Geary watched, a diesel shunting-engine came down the line into the station, pulling some empty coaches. As the wheels rolled over the lines they picked up the fresh, clinging snow, and when they had gone the metals were naked again, shining dully against the whiteness of the sleepers. Patiently, the snow began to cover them. Geary watched in a trance of enjoyment. He was standing on the last few inches of dry platform. Immediately in front of him, the snow lay in a ragged fringe. Isolated flakes drifted in and stuck to his coat and shoes.

To Geary, the snow seemed gentle, reassuring. As it settled on the high glass roof above him, it made the station as tranquil as a thatched cottage. By dimming the light and at the same time diffusing it more evenly through the atmosphere, it softened the outline of everything and made Geary feel that he was moving in a dream, not just any dream but one of those dreams in which we feel that our offences are forgiven and that all will be well.

At last he turned to walk back down the platform. As he did so he saw a knot of people at the far end, peering over one another's shoulders at something he could not clearly make out. Geary decided to avoid them. He enjoyed crowds, but only if they were vague and somnambulistic, mere fortuitous gatherings of individuals. This crowd at the bottom end of the platform, though small, seemed disquietingly full of purpose. It had obviously come together to do something, even if only to stare. Geary climbed the steps leading up to the bridge which spanned the top end of the station. He decided to walk right over to the far end and come down the platform at the other side. In that way, he could keep well away from that small, scuffling crowd.

As Geary went up the steps, the chief cameraman asked Adrian Swarthmore, 'D'you want us to go on filming?'

'No, hold it,' said Swarthmore. 'We'll get some more shots later. Can we have a telescopic lens for the next lot?'

'What are you doing?' one of the onlookers asked.

'Just taking some pictures of the station,' said Swarthmore. 'Routine film background.'

The crowd began to melt away now that filming had stopped. The chief cameraman consulted briefly with his laconic, sweatered crew.

'There he is,' said Swarthmore suddenly. 'Now, look, he's coming back down that platform on the far side.'

'If you want that shot, we can get the telescopics on him right away, from here.'

'Yes, I do. I do.'

As Geary reached the foyer end of the platform he looked across and saw that the object round which the crowd had clustered was a film camera. Its lens was pointed in his direction and as far as he could tell it was in action at that moment. He quickened his pace, not because he had any idea that he himself was the camera's target, but because he instinctively distrusted anything as disruptive as publicity. He wanted no part in any stunt that was going on, anything that might draw invidious attention to any part of the happily anonymous and amorphous life of the station. He hated the camera, the cluster of people round it, and the general air of excitement and unusualness. Walking fast, he pushed open the door of the refreshment room and went in.

There, life was going on as usual. None of the people sitting about, eating buns and drinking tea and coffee, seemed aware that there was anything happening outside. One man had removed his overcoat and was shaking snow from it: another was slowly unwinding a long muffler. The steamy cavern offered Geary exactly the indifferent, tranquil atmosphere he needed. Ordering coffee, he sank into a chair and opened a magazine. As he read, the disturbance faded from his mind and he became peaceful and cheerful again. This lasted for a few minutes, and then was shattered by the entry of two men who were discussing, loudly and combatively, the question of who the film people were and what they were doing. Others joined in, and soon no part of the refreshment room was out of range of the discussion. People kept making short excursions to see whether the filmmakers were still there, and coming back and reporting: they were there, they had disappeared, they had reappeared on a different part of the platform, they had gone into the hotel, they had come out again. . . . Finally, Geary folded his magazine, put it in his pocket, and stood up, glancing at his watch. He had a plan.

In two or three minutes a big express was due in from the west of England. Geary knew that a large crowd would come off the train and spill through the ticket barrier. Many of them would go straight to the underground railway. Geary decided to mingle with this crowd, go down into the underground station, stay there for as long as he felt comfortable, and then come up, by which time the film people would probably have packed up and gone.

This plan he carried out. The train was punctual. Geary was waiting for it by the barrier; he allowed the first few people to go by and only began to move when the crowd on either side of him had thickened. In this way he moved towards the underground with a mass bodyguard all round him. The crowd poured itself in a slow, viscous manner across the station foyer and down the broad stairs of the tube entrance. Geary floated among them, down a long corridor with a metal railing in the middle. He found himself among ticket-machines. For a moment he thought of taking a ticket and perhaps riding round the Inner Circle a few times, but this impulse quickly passed. The tube was unknown territory. He did not feel safe at any point on its huge system. There were crowds there, but they were not the sleep-walking, incurious crowds of the main-line station. The underground was part of London; if he went wandering in it he would hear the drums again.

Geary stood quite still beside one of the ticket-machines. People came and put money into it and pulled out tickets. One or two of them stared briefly at the man in his dark felt hat standing beside the machine, but most of them seemed not to notice him. If they registered him at all they probably assumed that he was waiting for someone.

When his watch showed that he had waited below ground for twenty minutes, Geary decided to get back to the station. The film people had probably gone by now, or at least moved to a different point. It should be possible to find a place where he would be undisturbed.

He went back down the long corridor, on the other side of the railing this time, and cautiously mounted the steps to the station foyer. He moved unobtrusively, neither too fast nor too slowly, and kept his eyes down. Swarthmore was waiting at the top of the steps. He had been worrying himself sick ever since Geary had gone down, but he had taken a chance and restrained himself from rushing in pursuit, team and all. Now his decision was justified and he breathed deeply in relief, at the same time moving into Geary's path and forcing him to stop.

'Ah, Mr. Geary,' he said genially. 'We meet again. It's funny, isn't it, how every time I come to the station I seem to run into you.'

'Yes,' said Geary. He moved sideways.

'I wonder if you'd mind,' said Swarthmore, shifting so as to keep in front of Geary, 'if I engaged you in a few minutes' conversation.'

Geary looked up at him for the first time. 'Conversation?'

'Yes. You see, I'm doing an article on the passenger railway service in the south-east. It may sound a trivial subject, but it affects a lot of people, and the article will be syndicated in all the chain of local papers in which I have a controlling interest.' When telling a lie, make it circumstantial, load it with detail. 'I'm asking a number of people who travel regularly what they think of the services in and out of London.'

'They're quite all right,' said Geary, trying to get past.

'Let's discuss it, anyway,' Swarthmore urged. 'Look, if you're not actually hurrying for a train now, shall we have a drink together in the hotel?'

'I'd rather do it some other time,' said Geary courteously.

'I may not be here another time,' said Swarthmore. He was conscious of the weight of the tape-recorder in his coat pocket. The knowledge that it was slowly revolving its neat little eardrums, taking down everything that was said, gave him the slightly breathless feeling of being in the presence of power; not exactly wielding power, nor exactly being wielded by it, but being in its lovely presence.

'No, really,' Geary was saying, when Swarthmore took his arm and, with laughing firmness, steered him into the buffet.

'Never mind the hotel,' said Swarthmore. 'This is quicker.'

Geary stood by the bar, looking intently at Swarthmore's face. When Swarthmore asked him what he would have to drink, he made no reply, but kept his eyes steadily on their target. As in their previous meeting, Swarthmore had the unnerving sensation that he, the hunter, was becoming the prey. Had Geary spotted the tape-recorder? Had he divined the whole scheme, cameras and all? The barmaid was standing looking at him, with her fingers drumming: he must give an order.

'Two whiskies, please,' he said, switching on a smile. As he spoke he turned his head, and when he turned it again he saw Geary's back. He was walking out.

'Oh, I say,' Swarthmore gasped, striding after him. 'Have I offended you?' He put a hand on Geary's shoulder. 'I'm sorry—I thought you wouldn't mind spending a few minutes of your time having a drink with me.' He wondered whether to smile and play it lightly, but his face, of its own accord, fell into reproachful creases, and he let them stay.

Geary halted. With the plump hand still on his shoulder, he half-turned his body and looked into Swarthmore's face with that same curious intentness, saying nothing.

'I just thought,' Swarthmore said nervously, 'what a lucky chance it was, meeting you twice in three days, and on the station both times. It seemed to . . . well, to call for a drink.' He smiled and let his hand fall from Geary's shoulder.

'They do say,' said Geary without expression, 'that if you hang about a big London station for long enough, you'll see everyone you've ever known.'

Swarthmore laughed in quick agreement. 'Certainly. But it isn't everyone you feel like asking to have a drink. I did feel like asking you and I'm sorry if I was over-insistent.'

'I thought you wanted to ask me my opinions for your article.'

'Well, I did, among other things, but that can wait. I mean, if you're averse to the idea that what you say might find its way into a newspaper article, we'll—'

'What I'm averse to,' said Geary, 'is being persecuted.'

'I'm sorry.'

Geary turned and walked out on to the platform. Swarthmore went slowly back to the bar. The two whiskies were ready and the woman was waiting to be paid. Silently, he handed over the money, poured one of the drinks into the other, and gulped them down.

Outside, Geary walked rapidly across the station foyer and into

the hotel. He summoned the lift and went straight to his room.
There, with the door safely locked, he took off his overcoat and
lay down on the bed with his face turned towards the window.
He could see a slab of heavy grey sky, framed in the oblong of
the window, and snowflakes whirling down. The flakes of snow
looked dark against the grey of the sky. They fell on and on, effort-
less and unstoppable, like a man's fate. Geary rolled on to his back
and looked up at the ceiling, which was also grey and had a meaningless plaster pattern. The pattern might have had some meaning
if he could have seen it all, but his room had been partitioned off
so as to make one large room into two smaller ones, and all he
could see was half the pattern. That half had itself been thrown
out of equilibrium by the installing of an electric light which had
not been originally planned for. After a few minutes the mean-
inglessness and imbalance of the ceiling pattern made Geary feel
oppressed and ill. He turned back for a moment to the oblong of
sky and the falling snowflakes, then got up and paced about the
room. His hands and forehead were damp with sweat, and his
chest was itching under the clinging plaster. Far away, the drums
started beating.

Going to the dressing-table, he took out his flask and poured
some whisky into his tooth-glass. He stood in front of the mirror,
looking at himself and drinking, then poured out some more and
drank that. The whisky steadied him, and he put the bottle away,
got into his overcoat and went to the door. Carefully, he opened it
a little way. Nobody was about in the corridor. Geary went softly
along to the lift, entered it and closed the gates. For an instant he
leaned against the side of the lift with his eyes closed. Then he
pressed the button for the ground floor.

The chief cameraman, his hands deep in his thick overcoat with
the turned-up collar, sat on the bench that ran along the wall of
the waiting-room, and kicked his heels on the woodwork behind
him. All around, his youthful assistants fidgeted and smoked.
Swarthmore stood in the middle of the room, holding the tape
recorder in his hand. The two film cameras stood on the table,

each with its dark monocle fixed on Swarthmore's face with an unbearable irony.

'What if he doesn't come out?' said the chief cameraman.

'He'll come out,' said Swarthmore. 'And if he doesn't, we'll sit where we are and you'll get paid for a full day's work, with overtime if necessary, and you won't have to do a stroke.'

'I'd rather be at home,' said the chief cameraman, 'and sod the overtime. I'm definitely sickening for something.'

Swarthmore flushed with anger. He felt that the chief cameraman despised him. The three young men in their thick sweaters also despised him, but that was different; it was merely automatic; they would have despised anyone who was fat and middle-aged and did not compel their respect by a demonstrable mastery of some technique. Swarthmore could put up with that, but he felt that the head cameraman, who was of his own generation, despised him because he was spying on a man, eavesdropping on him with a hidden tape-recorder and a telescopic lens, prying into the secret of how he lived his life and sheltered his nakedness, and for no better motive than to confide this secret importantly across the hearthrug in a million living-rooms he would never visit.

'His defences are pretty good, of course,' he said. 'He's adept at seeming normal. But the more strangely he acts, the more necessary it is to draw attention to it and get him the help he needs.'

'Why not just send for a doctor?' said the chief cameraman in his flat accent.

At that moment Swarthmore was very close to giving up. His mouth was ready to open and say that they would pack up and go and leave Geary to sort it out for himself. Then he saw an uncannily clear mental picture of Sir Ben Warble, tapping the ash off his cigar and smiling at him across that bare desk. A scoop! That was how Ben would smile at him—his eyes hooded, derisive—when he had to go to him and admit that the much-needed scoop had simply not turned up. 'What happened to that mad scientist you found on Paddington Station?' he could hear Sir Ben asking. And himself replying, 'We let him go. It seemed a shame to pester him.' No, he could never say that and face Ben's pitying smile.

He hated the head cameraman for despising him, but he hated

Geary much worse, because Geary was the prime mover. If Geary had not gone out of his mind and taken to living on the station, then he, Swarthmore, would not find himself compelled to behave contemptibly. If Geary would only complete the job and run mad altogether, it would be different. They could get a few good shots of him being pinioned and laced into a strait-jacket by men in white coats, and all would be well. He would be congratulated on his good luck and good timing in being on the spot with a camera crew all ready. But Geary was spoiling it all by being mad in such a decorous way, walking calmly about the station and doing no harm to anybody.

Swarthmore stood motionless on the damp floor of the waiting-room and silently cursed Geary with deep, inward curses full of real hate. He felt that Geary had trapped him in an impossible situation which must end in pain and humiliation for one or other of them.

'If he doesn't come out in ten minutes,' he said between his teeth, 'I'm going into that hotel to get him.'

'Why not let the poor bugger alone?' said the chief cameraman.

'He's got to be watched anyway,' said Swarthmore. 'Leave him alone, and the next thing you know he'll run amok and murder somebody.'

Frowning, he sat down heavily and began to stare at his watch, trying to catch the minute-hand in the act of moving. Sometimes he fancied he saw it move, but he could not keep his attention fixed on it steadily enough. The watch seemed to smile up at him contemptuously, like Sir Ben. He thought of Angela Geary's long, bronze hair, he thought of the *Showcase* team interviewing African politicians at the airport, and he thought briefly of the snow falling outside on the streets and the railway lines. Then he noticed that the ten minutes were up.

'Better have the cameras ready,' he said. 'I'll get him out on to the platform, but I can't predict what'll happen after that.'

Buttoning his coat, he left the waiting-room and walked over to the hotel entrance. As he pushed open the door he wondered what he was going to do. It was like watching someone else, some stranger whose actions he could not predict. Was he really going to go to the desk and ask for Geary? If he did, they would presumably telephone Geary's room; what would happen if Geary did not answer? He must try to find out the room number. Perhaps the girl would ask the switchboard for it and he would be able to overhear her. Or perhaps he could get a glance at the register. Then he could wait till nobody was looking at him and take the lift up and knock on Geary's door. Geary would think it was some hotel servant and open the door.

And then? What would this stranger do then?

Still wondering, Swarthmore went into the hotel lobby. There, sitting in an armchair with his overcoat still on and his dark felt hat on a small table beside him, was Geary. Geary must have felt Swarthmore's eyes on him, because he looked up at once.

Swarthmore stopped dead. Now that Geary was suddenly there, now that it had turned out so absurdly easy to find him, he did not know what to say or do.

Nobody could have known it, but in the struggle between the two men victory was in Geary's grasp. He sat quite still, ready to stare Swarthmore down. If he had done so, Swarthmore would have gone away and taken his hate and his clammy anxiety and his self-loathing somewhere else. But as Geary sat in the armchair amid the discreet lighting of the hotel foyer, he was suddenly hit by the one thing he could not defend himself against. He heard the drums again.

Geary knew at once that if Swarthmore had the power to start the drums going, it was useless to stand and confront him. He got up at once and walked quickly out of the hotel on the street side. A taxi was passing, and he thought of hailing it and making his escape into the unmapped wilderness of London. But the drums drove him back. More quickly still, he walked round the side of the hotel and back towards the station. It is an architectural peculiarity of Paddington Station that it does not have what could be described as a main entrance. The whole front façade is occupied by the hotel, and if you walk on to the station you always do so from the side. It is as if Brunel liked trains better than human beings: the trains enter like queens under the high steel arches. Geary, half-running, entered the station by means of the paltry little street that runs down below the advertisement hoardings.

Away on the other side of the foyer, the chief cameraman and his crew had come out on to the platform and were at the ready. Swarthmore, following close behind Geary, summoned them into action with a great wave of his arm. At once the chief cameraman began filming with one camera, while two of his assistants picked up the other camera and its tripod and hurried after Swarthmore. Geary, turning his head, saw all this, and at once broke away sharply to the right, crossing over in front of the taxi-rank. He was making for the non-public part of the station.

The long platform, littered with sacks and bales, bounded by the dark line of cave-entrances, seemed to offer immunity from the drums. Geary broke into a run. Leaving Swarthmore behind, he raced along two-thirds of the length of the platform. The shadows received him with hospitality. The high electric lamps, pale in the quiet subaqueous light caused by the snow, did not probe down far enough to question Geary as he hurried in his dark overcoat. Safety: he swung round a loaded wagon and ran into one of the caverns.

He stopped. Facing him, one hand gripping a long-handled broom on which his square-cut body was partly leaning, stood the porter, Charley. When he saw that the intruder was Geary, Charley's face broke into a smile full of triumph and menace. He grasped his broom as if it were a pike, and moved forward.

Geary thought he saw Charley's lips move, but he caught no words; they were drowned in the frenzy of the drums. He retreated. The platform was empty except for the advancing figure of Swarthmore, who was followed in turn by the two young men with their camera. Swarthmore, in his excitement, cried 'Hi!' as if Geary were a thief. Geary turned, dodged among the taxis, and ran towards the stairs that led up to the bridge.

Taxi-drivers, reading newspapers as they waited to start their engines, turned their heads to watch the chase that suddenly materialized among them. Geary, his dark felt hat still decorously on his head, ran up the steps on to the bridge. Swarthmore galloped after him. Most of the people on the station were unaware that anything was happening. Away in the foyer, the chief cameraman, having lost sight of Geary, stopped his camera and waited, wishing himself at home.

As he crossed the bridge, Geary slowed down to a firm walk. He had decided what to do. During his many hours of strolling about the station, he had become very well acquainted with its physical construction, and he knew that it was an easy matter, even for a middle-aged man, to lower himself from the bridge on to the roof of Platform Two. The high domes of the main glass roof come to an end about two-thirds of the way along the platforms, which are sheltered for their remaining length by ordinary curving metal roofs like those at any country station. Geary calculated that if he could get on to the roof of Platform Two, the easiest one to reach, he could leave Swarthmore safely behind. Swarthmore would be out of voice-range, and he could scarcely bellow questions at him through a megaphone.

Firm in his decision, Geary walked sedately to the point at which he intended to leave the bridge. Although he knew that Swarthmore must be close behind him, he held himself so casually that a fat man in a mackintosh, coming across the bridge the opposite way, passed him without a glance. The fat man was walking with long, energetic strides and swinging a full brief-case in his right hand: he was out to do a good day's business. Geary slowed down even further to let him get well past. Then, with deliberate and economical movements, he reached up, grasped a conveniently situated iron lamp-bracket that curved down to meet him, put his other hand on the broad steel parapet of the bridge, and pulled himself up.

Steadying himself with one hand against a roof-pillar which soared up beside him, Geary climbed down on to a flat girder, moved easily along it, skirted another pillar, and dropped lightly on to the roof of Platform Two.

Adrian Swarthmore, following behind him, was nonplussed when he saw Geary climb up on to the parapet. A stifled exclamation escaped him. The fat man, by now abreast of Swarthmore, halted and looked at him in surprise. Swarthmore, seeing Geary move purposefully out along the girder, broke into a run. 'Here, come back,' he said. For some reason he did not want to shout. He had an obscure feeling that if he could keep the whole scene quiet, prevent Geary from attracting a crowd, everything would remain under control. As Geary dropped down on to the roof of Platform Two, Swarthmore hurried up to the point at which Geary had climbed over the parapet, and leaned over. Above him was the end façade of the great glass roof; below, the long platforms with their snow-covered Dutch-barn lids. Geary was under the open sky; snow had already begun to speckle his overcoat and his dark hat.

'Geary,' Swarthmore called, his voice urgent but cautious. 'Come back. You'll kill yourself.'

Geary stood impassively looking at him from a distance of some twenty yards. Swarthmore felt utterly impotent. He had no intention of climbing after Geary; for one thing it was dangerous, and for another he was sure there must be a law against it. If the man had run mad and decided to go clambering about the roofs, let the police get him down.

Geary could not be seen from the platform below him, but people on the other platforms were beginning to notice him and to move up to positions where they had a better view. Suddenly Swarthmore noticed that the chief cameraman was among them. He was setting up his camera, and as Swarthmore watched he focused it and began to film. At the same instant, the two young men with the second camera came hurrying up beside Swarthmore, and without waiting for instructions balanced their camera on the parapet of the bridge and began filming also. Geary was caught and held in the sight-beams of the two contrivances.

Without hesitation he turned and walked along the centre of the platform roof, out towards the end, with his back to the station. The cameras followed him: the one on the platform swivelled its square black head, the one on the parapet merely lifted its snout a little. Geary walked fast amid the thick-falling snowflakes. His feet left tracks which immediately began to be covered up.

Reaching the end, he stood for a moment outlined against the open sky. The small crowds on the two adjacent platforms had moved along with him step by step, and now they halted with him. There seemed nowhere to go, and Geary began to hear the drums more loudly than ever, so that their thundering seemed to shake

his chest inside its coating of plaster. The plaster was due to come
off in three days' time, and Geary found himself wondering what
would happen between now and then. It was Wednesday: how
would he get through till Saturday? How would he come down off
this roof? He looked forward very much to getting the plaster off,
but he could not imagine Saturday. Would it still be morning then?

A policeman had appeared among the crowd on his left, and
people were pointing up at Geary and explaining. He wondered
what reasons they were giving for his being on the roof. The
policeman began to call to him in a stern voice, but Geary paid
no attention. He stood looking out along the snow-covered lines
for a minute and then turned and began to walk back towards the
great glass arches. As he walked, a train going to some unremark-
able place pulled out along the line from Platform Five. It was full
of people opening newspapers and settling where to put their
feet. That evening, perhaps, they would read in the papers that a
man had walked along a platform roof at Paddington, and would
think how they had just missed seeing him, and for a moment they
would feel important, brushed by the sleeve of great events.

The cameras followed Geary as he went back along the platform roof. Adrian Swarthmore was still staring incredulously at
him from the bridge. The situation had left Swarthmore behind.
He had no idea what to do. Events would carry him along and he
was content that they should. And beneath his contentment was
a shocked pity for Geary: and beneath the pity a dark, wild joy.
Geary had done what was necessary, he had justified the whole
expedition, the chief cameraman would not despise him any more
and Sir Ben would agree to take him on. He would be a success.
Geary would make a success of him.

Geary's face was closed and preoccupied as he came back down
the platform roof. At first, Swarthmore thought he intended to
get back over the parapet on to the bridge. He looked at the two
young men beside him, serious in their thick sweaters, intent on
nothing but tending their cruel, impersonal instrument. Their
presence reassured Swarthmore. With their aid, it should not be
difficult to hold Geary until a policeman could take him in charge.
Perhaps it would be worth trying to hold him without their help:

they could go on filming and it would make a wonderful shot. TV Personality Grapples with Mad Scientist. See it actually happening on your screen. He slipped off his overcoat ready for the struggle.

Geary, however, did not come back to the bridge. When he reached the end of the platform roof, he pulled himself up till he was level with the point where Swarthmore stood, watching. But instead of coming back along the girder that led to the parapet of the bridge, he suddenly swung himself up on to the narrow strip of metal running along the front of the main façade of the station roof with its huge metal-and-glass arches. Then, deliberately, he moved on to the narrow passage between the two main arches, in the very centre of the roof.

What Geary had in mind was to walk along this central path until he reached the foyer end of the station. Then, somehow or other, he would make his way down, and peaceably give himself up. He had no objection to being interviewed by a policeman, even arrested. He knew it was illegal to clamber about on the station roof, that it created a disturbance and set a bad example to young people. He was quite willing to be summoned to a magistrate's court and fined five or ten pounds. He could come back to the station afterwards and all would be well and he would be safe from the drums. It was the cameras that made the drums beat so loudly. He had to get away from the cameras because of the way they stared at him and drew human eyes after him, so that he was being questioned, questioned, questioned all the time.

Geary climbed on to the central metal strip, between the two arches, on his hands and knees. Then he stood upright and began to walk, without haste, back down the length of the roof. But only for a couple of steps. With the drums thundering, he halted. His memory had been at fault. After all those hundreds of hours of strolling about the station, observing its features, he had still not grasped—not until this dreadful moment—that the arches forming the roof are not continuous. They are interrupted at two points by steel columns and high glass domes. It is not possible to walk along the whole length of the roof, even on the secure footing of the cat-walk between the central arches. For this, too, is twice interrupted by the high glass domes.

Geary stood absolutely still. No one could see him. The arches of Paddington station are made of glass only above a certain point. Up to that point, they are of metal. A man standing between the arches cannot be seen from below, and if he keeps away from the far end he cannot be seen from any angle. So Geary stood, breathing quietly, the snow falling on to him from a softly luminous sky. He looked up at the sky, relishing its pearliness. It seemed bigger, more welcoming, than it had ever been before. All at once he felt that the station had outlived its usefulness to him. He wanted to walk freely under this vast open sky, to look up into it, to receive its blessings. The station had been essential to him when he needed a smaller sky, one that would fit over his world like a protecting lid. But now he needed the real sky, the immeasurable generosity of space.

He kept still, no longer willing to give himself up, but also no longer afraid. He decided that if he kept quite still for a sufficient length of time, the cameras would go away, the crowds would disperse, and he could make his way down and leave the station quietly. He saw himself, with exultation, packing in his hotel room, then coming down and paying the bill and leaving. To some place in the country. Waking up in a country inn, to the sound of cock-crow, and looking out of the window and seeing the sky big and clear. Clouds piled up, touched with gold by the sun, moving in their unalterable direction. He was free at last. He had a clear, sunlit vision of two figures walking across a broad open field: a man and a boy: himself and David. Then the loudspeakers started.

'THIS IS A MESSAGE TO THE MAN WHO IS AT PRESENT ON THE MAIN ROOF OF THE STATION. IN THE INTERESTS OF YOUR OWN AND OTHER PEOPLE'S SAFETY WE ASK YOU TO COME DOWN AT ONCE.'

It was a good idea on someone's part, to use the public address system of the station to get in touch with the unclassifiable man who was not a traveller, not a trainspotter, not waiting, but simply standing on the roof and by that simple act challenging the whole sane and sturdy world of trains, time-tables, business journeys and newsstands. The self-assured voice went on, in a matter-of-fact sub-Cockney intonation, to reassure the public. There was no danger. No one had any reason to believe that the man on the roof was a criminal, or that he was armed or in any way dangerous. Several police officers were standing by, just in case, but as far as anyone knew he was just a member of the public who had taken it into his head to go climbing.

Then the voice turned back to Geary: 'ONCE AGAIN WE ADDRESS THE MAN WHO IS AT PRESENT SOMEWHERE BETWEEN THE TWO CENTRAL ARCHES OF THE MAIN ROOF. PLEASE COME DOWN OR YOU WILL HAVE TO BE FETCHED DOWN.'

The loudspeakers clicked off, and the station was held in a tense silence. Not even a diesel purred, not even a trolley clanked. Everyone was listening and watching for Geary. He understood this, but he did not know what to do. He could not come down, into reach of all the cameras and all the eyes. He needed to get away by himself, to some place where the sky was big and the drums would never be heard.

The silence was good, but he knew that at any moment the public address system would begin calling to him again, and a silence that is just about to be broken is as bad as a noise. He had to move, before that mechanical voice began again, and the only way to go was up. He suddenly launched himself forward, climbing steeply, clawing at the tiles. There was just enough purchase for his feet and hands to thrust him upward, and as he climbed higher the slope grew less acute and he was able to let go with his hands and straighten up. He moved on: the tiles gave way to glass, but he did not falter. A great crack appeared under his feet: he shifted his weight on to a fresh pane just in time, but there was another crack, another, another, and as Geary reached the highest point and put his weight squarely on the glass, it gave way with a splintering sound that echoed in every corner of the station. There was nothing to hold Geary and he fell, turning over on to his back as he made a last effort to hold on.

It seemed to Geary that he fell for a long time. Landing on his back on the metals, he broke his spine and fractured his skull in the same instant. His body made one great writhing movement, as if he were trying to get up, but this must have been nothing more than a reflex on the part of the already dead nerves. As he fell back across the lines, his dark felt hat rolled off and lay beside him, open to the sky like a begging-bowl.

As Geary died, two good things happened. The drums ceased, and the snow went on falling.

NEW AND FORTHCOMING TITLES FROM
VALANCOURT BOOKS

FRANCIS KING	To the Dark Tower
	Never Again
	An Air That Kills
	The Dividing Stream
	The Dark Glasses
	The Man on the Rock
C.H.B. KITCHIN	Ten Pollitt Place
	The Book of Life
HILDA LEWIS	The Witch and the Priest
KENNETH MARTIN	Aubade
	Waiting for the Sky to Fall
MICHAEL NELSON	Knock or Ring
	A Room in Chelsea Square
BEVERLEY NICHOLS	Crazy Pavements
OLIVER ONIONS	The Hand of Kornelius Voyt
DENNIS PARRY	Sea of Glass
J.B. PRIESTLEY	Benighted
	The Other Place
	The Magicians
PETER PRINCE	Play Things
PIERS PAUL READ	Monk Dawson
FORREST REID	The Garden God
	Following Darkness
	The Spring Song
	Brian Westby
	The Tom Barber Trilogy
	Denis Bracknel
DAVID STOREY	Radcliffe
	Pasmore
	Saville
RUSSELL THORNDIKE	The Slype
	The Master of the Macabre
JOHN TREVENA	Sleeping Waters
JOHN WAIN	Hurry on Down
KEITH WATERHOUSE	There is a Happy Land
	Billy Liar
COLIN WILSON	Ritual in the Dark
	Man Without a Shadow
	The World of Violence
	The Philosopher's Stone
	The God of the Labyrinth

Lightning Source UK Ltd.
Milton Keynes UK
UKOW040253150613

212307UK00002B/31/P